TORI

THE BEST SUMMER

Diane McClure Jones

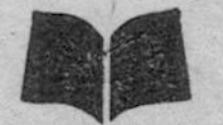

SCHOLASTIC BOOK SERVICES
New York Toronto London Auckland Sydney Tokyo

Cover Photo by Owen Brown

ISBN 0-590-31933-7

12 11 10 9 8 7 6 5 4 3 2 2 3 4 5 6 7/8

Printed in the U.S.A. 06

TORI

THE BEST SUMMER

A Wildfire Book

WILDFIRE TITLES FROM SCHOLASTIC

Chapter 1

Tori Baniff brushed her fingers through her unruly hair. She scowled at her image in the long mirror that covered the width of the girls' lavatory at Lincoln High. Darn, she'd forgotten her comb again.

Sonja Delaney, Miss Homecoming, head cheerleader and all-around easy winner for any beauty contest, pushed her way to the mirror, shoving aside the other girls. When she slid her books onto the ledge beneath the mirror, she knocked off Shirl Clarke's purse. The contents spilled across the floor. Tori squatted down, grabbed the pencils, combs, wallet, tucked them back in the purse, and handed it to Shirl. Shirl's lip quivered.

Tori stood slowly until her gaze met Sonja's in the mirror. A curl of acrid smoke drifted up from a forbidden cigarette, propped on the ledge in front of Sonja. Most of the students who broke the school's no-smoking rule did their smoking in the cubicles. It was typical of Sonja's nerve to leave her cigarette in sight of everyone.

Sonja smiled sweetly and said, "Is my smoke bothering you?"

Tori smiled just as sweetly and let her gaze sweep down Sonja's full figure, then return to meet her eyes. In her clear voice, Tori said, "No, and I am relieved to see that it hasn't stunted your growth."

As Tori held the heavy door to the corridor open for Shirl, she heard the snickers echoing off the tiled walls. Someone whispered, "The Mouth strikes again."

Tori and Shirl wandered down the hall toward their first class, making their way between locker doors and other students. Tori was relieved to see that Shirl was smiling now, the threat of tears gone.

Shirl Clarke was a small girl for her sixteen years, with a pale, heart-shaped face and thin, wispy blonde hair. A spinal birth defect caused her constant backaches and made it difficult to bend. Shirl tried hard to ignore her problem so that others would not know about it. An incident like the one with Sonja could leave her with crushed feelings for the rest of the day.

A group of freshmen boys elbowed each other into the traffic flow, one of them sailing full force into Tori.

"Ouch!" Tori yelled.

Clutching her books in one arm, she caught the boy around the shoulders with her free arm. His shocked red face was only a few inches from hers, his eyes on the same level. He mumbled a confused, "Sorry."

Tori flashed her wide grin and said loudly, "Me, too, sweetie, because you're awfully cute, but I never rob cradles."

His friends hooted.

The boy's eyes widened. Tori pushed him gently back toward his friends. His gaze followed her as she and Shirl crossed the hall to join a group of juniors outside the civics room.

Shirl said, "Tori, he's still watching you."

When the other girls turned to see what Shirl was talking about, Tori said, "That's as it should be, Shirl. Freshmen are *supposed* to worship juniors, right?"

Tori struck a model's pose, body twisted, one hip jutted out, free arm bent upward over her head. Her jeans and orange T-shirt clung to her slim shape. Raising her chin to show the group her profile, she said loudly, "Can you wonder that a mere freshman is dazzled? Get a look at that next contestant, folks! Presenting Miss Victoria Baniff! Average height, average weight, average hair-colored hair, nothing sticking out where it shouldn't and nothing sticking out where it should! Square face, square jaw, Silly Putty nose, but dig the classy orthodontics and the big brown eyes!"

When the bell rang, Tori's friends were still laughing. They hurried into the civics room, pushing past a couple of boys who blocked the doorway, and slid behind their desks. Tori spread her books out on the desk, rummaging wildly through her folder. Wrinkled papers fell from it. When she finally found her assignment, she slapped it on top of her books, stuffed the rest of her papers noisily back into the folder, and relaxed into her seat with a loud sigh.

The silence in the room reached her. She looked up into Mr. Brown's face.

The teacher was a tall, heavy man with an unreadable expression. He said carefully, "Are you quite ready, Victoria?"

Tori flashed her grin and said, "Yessir, you may start class now."

"Thank you so much," he said.

Tori kept her eyes on him, afraid to look away, because behind her confident smile she hid a few doubts. Mr. Brown was not a pushover. Unlike some of her teachers, he would take only so much interruption in his class and then he would expel a student. The trouble was that no one could guess when he was approaching his boiling point. Tori constantly studied him for signs — a narrowing of the eyes, stiffening of the spine, or clenching of fists — sure indications in other teachers that she was pushing her luck. But Mr. Brown never gave away a hint.

When Mr. Brown turned to the blackboard, Tori slumped down in her seat. She let her hands dangle at her sides, as though she had had a reprieve, knowing the class watched her. She was rewarded by appreciative giggling from the back row.

Pretending not to notice, she concentrated on the board, its surface pale in the light that streamed through the windows. The room smelled of chalk dust and floor wax, as well as the odor of the bananas in the brown bag lunches that had been jammed into book-filled backpacks.

Tori felt a folded slip of paper being pressed into her dangling hand. She closed her fingers over it just as Mr. Brown turned back to face the class. Widening her large brown eyes in what she hoped was an expression of rapt attention, Tori kept her gaze on the teacher while her hand moved slowly to her lap to open the note. As soon as Mr. Brown moved to the other side of the room, she looked down and read, "Same today?" printed in block letters.

Turning slowly in her chair, Tori glanced at the far corner, saw Dom Hallett in his seat by the wall, and winked at him.

His note meant, "Will you meet me in the cafeteria at noon and help me with the algebra assignment?"

Her wink definitely meant "Yes."

Sometimes when Tori helped Dom with Algebra 3, she suspected that he did not need help. She hoped that was the case. If it was, then he asked for help because he wanted to be with her rather than because he did not understand algebra.

Tori definitely wanted to be with Dom. There were two kinds of boys who always sat near the back of classrooms, she had noticed. The first type was the turkeys, boys who spent twelve years staring at classroom ceilings, not caring if the teacher called on them. They didn't mind saying, "I dunno." The other type was smart enough, but they hoped the teacher wouldn't notice them because they didn't like to answer out loud. Tori had known several of the second type, and they were always nice boys, polite and even-tempered, but very shy.

That was Dom. He was nice, polite, good-natured. More than that, he was tall, long-legged, and had a pleasant oval face with friendly blue eyes and a shy smile. His light hair fell back in soft waves from his face to lie neatly in place. She also envied his slightly arched nose. It had real bone and shape to it, not like her pug nose.

As far as she knew, Dom did not have a girlfriend. If he did, she would have heard by now. Shirl knew who were a couple, who had been a couple, and even who were going to be a couple. Lincoln High had only six hundred students, and everyone knew everyone since kindergarten, so Shirl could easily keep all her information straight. Besides that, Shirl spent a couple of evenings a week with her boyfriend-since-fifth-grade, Cowboy Everson, and still earned above-average grades.

Mr. Brown said, "Bill, define a caucus."

Bill's face sagged. He said slowly, "Uh — uh — yeah, that's — oh, something like — you know — oh — I dunno."

Mr. Brown said, "Victoria, can you answer that question?"

"Wow, some people sure have dead cells in their batteries," Tori said, rolling her eyes in Bill's direction. "A caucus is a meeting of party members to choose delegates to pick candidates."

When Mr. Brown nodded, Tori couldn't resist adding, "Right again, huh?"

Ignoring Tori's remark, Mr. Brown went on to the next question. Tori had thought he would smile. Instead his expression remained calm and unreadable. Was he getting near his blowup point? Tori bit her lip and decided she had better cool it in his class for a few days.

At noon Tori and Shirl were the first to reach their table. The cafeteria was divided into two sections, one end filled with long tables and benches for freshmen and sophomores, the other with round tables and chairs for the upper classmen. After pushing her books under her chair, Tori pulled her bag lunch out of her purse.

Shirl said, "You know, Tori, Bill really is dumb. I mean, he's not just lazy, he is really dumb."

Tori said, "Typical jock."

Shirl said slowly, "No, I don't think so. See, he can't help it that he isn't smart. I mean — I'm not sure — it doesn't seem quite fair to make fun of him if he can't help it."

Before Tori could answer, Cowboy swung his leg over his chair back and dropped into the seat on the other side of Shirl. Cowboy was one of those boys whose bones jutted out everywhere, all elbows, knees, skinny fingers, sharp nose and chin, and slightly crooked teeth in a slightly crooked smile. His pale skin glowed with freckles. His straight orange hair tumbled into his eyes.

Cowboy would have been called Red if it hadn't been for his talent. He lugged his guitar to every party, school assembly, or town gathering. His long hands danced over the strings, drawing out lively melodies while he rattled off the words in a brittle, singsong style. Folk and western songs were his best, earning him the nickname Cowboy.

Living up to his name, as usual, Cowboy drawled, "Howdy, little ladies."

Dom slammed his tray next to Tori. The noodles on his divided plate sloshed over into the Jello.

"I hope you aren't planning a career as a waiter," Tori said.

Dom smiled, sat down, and concentrated on opening his milk carton.

"Did you finish your work sheet?" Tori asked Dom. For some reason that she still couldn't figure out, she always spoke first to him. A few times she had waited, biting her lip to hold back her words, but after he had sat beside her in silence for more than thirty seconds, she always broke down and started the conversation.

"Uh huh. But I don't get the last problem." He dug a worn piece of paper from his hip pocket, unfolded it, and smoothed out the creases. Tori leaned toward him to read it.

"Not too close there," Cowboy said. "Keep it clean in the cafeteria."

"How would you like a banana peel for a hat?" Torn said without looking up. To Dom she said, "No, that problem is right down to there, but the answer is wrong. Umm. Wait a sec. I see. You've got the right formula. It's just an error in multiplication."

Dom said, "Damn, I wasted half an hour on that last night."

"You could have phoned me," Tori said, hoping she sounded very casual and not at all as though she would like him to phone her.

"Oh. Yeah. Well, I wouldn't want to bother you," Dom said. "I mean, if your family is having supper — or something."

"You can call between eight and ten," Tori said, staring hard at his paper and trying to keep her voice low so that no one else would hear. "All I'm doing then is studying."

When Dom didn't answer, Tori wasn't sure if he had heard her above the shouting and clatter of trays. She looked at him. He smiled. But then, Dom always smiled when she looked at him, a quick, shy smile that lit up his face.

Chapter 2

After the dismissal bell rang, Tori ran through the corridors to her locker, ducking around knots of people in the halls. She tossed her books and backpack into her locker, dragged out her paint clothes, and, while kicking at the pile of papers and scarves and books that threatened to slide out onto the floor, slammed the door shut. Its metal clang echoed down the corridor, matched by hundreds of other banging locker doors. Dodging through the sea of students who raced to catch the buses, Tori ran down the hall toward the auditorium.

A teacher called, "Don't run in the halls."

Tori shouted back, "Just warming up for cross-country," caught the auditorium door frame with her free hand, and skidded around the turn from the corridor to race up the steps past the stage.

The auditorium was a large multipurpose room, with seats installed on tiers to give a clear view of the stage and the movie screen that could be lowered in front of it. Each seat had a fold-down writing desk, allowing the room to be used as a lecture hall. Behind the stage were several storerooms for theater equipment and band instruments, plus two dressing rooms. There was a fire in the girls' dressing room wastebasket a month earlier, probably from a carelessly tossed cigarette. It had smoked up the walls so badly that the principal had decided, for disciplinary reasons, to lock the room for the rest of the school year. When this left the girls with no place to change their clothes, they moved into the boys' dressing room. Through force of numbers the girls won the teacher's okay, but the boys still disapproved.

As Tori approached, Cowboy and a couple of other boys were knocking on the dressing room door, shouting, "Hurry up in there."

"Gang way," Tori said, sticking out her elbows to shove between them.

"Shirl's already in there. How long you going to be?" Cowboy demanded.

"Eons."

"Aw, Tori! Come on, I've gotta try on my costume."

"Mrs. O told you guys to change behind the back curtain," Tori said.

"That's not fair! This is our room," Cowboy said.

Tori slipped past him and around the door, then stuck her head out to ask, "What's the matter, sweetie, you afraid somebody's gonna peek?"

She closed the door on Cowboy's howl of protest. Shirl pushed back into the row of old costumes to make room for Tori. She had already changed into her paint clothes. The dressing room was little more than a closet, with a clothes rod lining one wall and a narrow shelf and mirror on the other side. Tori switched into her paint-spattered jeans and sweatshirt, jamming her school clothes into her sack.

"Your werewolf is outside baring his fangs," Tori told Shirl. "If we lock him out of the dressing room much longer, he's going to bare a lot more."

Shirl laughed. "Not Cowboy. His mother gave him a fishnet shirt for his birthday and he won't wear it."

"Why? Does he think it's X-rated?"

"Something like that."

"I don't get it," Tori said. She sat on the edge of the shelf and tied the laces of her old tennis shoes. "You say he's so shy, but he isn't shy around you."

"That's different. I guess he feels comfortable with me."

"Is that what it takes to get a guy's attention? You have to make him think of you as a pair of old socks?" Tori spoke lightly, as though she were wisecracking, but Shirl saw through it.

"Trouble with Dom?" she asked.

"Don't I wish! How can he cause me trouble when he won't even phone?"

The boys banged with their fists, making the door rattle.

"Come on, before they break it down," Tori said. Catching the knob, she turned it and jerked the door inward. Cowboy let out a shriek. He fell past her into the clothes rack.

"That was a great entrance, Cowboy," Tori said sweetly as she led Shirl into the corridor. "If you can do that again on opening night, you'll steal the show."

"Get outta here!" was all Cowboy could reply as he freed himself from the tangle of fallen costumes.

"That's a very weak comeback," Tori called over her shoulder.

Canvas scenery flats were lined up against the back wall of the stage. Their brushes and paint cans had already been arranged on the drop cloth in front of the flats by Emily, the senior who had designed the sets and was in charge of the stage crew.

Tori studied the canvas-covered wood frames. One canvas contained a chalk outline drawing of a window in a wall. The words "white" were written on the windowsill and "yellow" on the wall. It was part of an interior scene of a parlor for the play. The other two flats were for an outdoor scene, their canvases covered with chalk outlines of trees and shrubbery and a picket fence, with the sky area labeled "blue."

Tori asked Shirl, "Would you rather be an interior decorator or God?"

"You sound like those career counseling questionnaires," Shirl said.

"They never give such clear choices."

"Ummm, maybe not. Well, I think I'll paint that window flat."

"Right. I'll play God and paint the trees," Tori said. She dipped her brush into the dark green paint and dabbed at the chalked leaf patterns. She had originally gone out for drama because she thought she would like to act, but found she enjoyed painting flats equally well. Although she had a good part in this play, she helped the stage crew on the afternoons that she wasn't scheduled to rehearse her scene.

A narrow line of green paint slid out from the leaf shape and glided down the canvas. Tori clutched at the waistband of her shirt, leaned forward and dabbed the streak of paint, managing to absorb a wide spot on her sweat shirt. But in leaning forward, her head brushed against the wet canvas.

"Look out," Shirl said, too late.

"Oh, hell," Tori muttered, rubbing at the green spot on her disheveled hair.

A crisp voice from the back of the auditorium asked, "Where is your paint rag, Tori? How many times have I told you people to always have a rag when you're painting?"

"My whole body is a rag," Tori complained.

Mrs. Odell, the drama coach, marched down the aisle, waving her sheaf of scripts. She was a tall woman with wide eyes, flowing blonde hair, and the kind of cheekbones fashion models covet. "Why are you painting today, anyway, Tori?"

"Because I am a good person," Tori said, as she grabbed Shirl's paint rag and rubbed at the spill. "I may not be a good artist, Mrs. O, but I am definitely a good person. Why else would anyone with so little talent for painting come down here every day to cover herself with paint?"

Mrs. Odell smiled. "That's not what I meant. Tori, you and Cowboy are scheduled to rehearse your musical number now."

Tori blurted, "My number with Cowboy? Today? That's not today, that's tomorrow!"

"Now, Tori, I keep telling you, and everyone

else, to check the rehearsal board," Mrs. Odell said in her clear stage voice.

"I did check the board. It lists my second act rehearsal with Cowboy for Wednesday."

"Exactly."

"But, Mrs. O, this is Tuesday."

The teacher's eyes widened. "Tuesday? This is Tuesday?"

"All day," Tori said.

Mrs. Odell wailed, "But I taught my Wednesday lesson plan today!"

"So teach your Tuesday plan tomorrow," Tori said.

"I'll have to, won't I, but that doesn't help rehearsals. No matter what day tomorrow is, I won't be here after school, so if I am going to watch you rehearse, you and Cowboy have to do it now. Is he around?"

Tori ran to the dressing room, banged on the door, and shouted, "Hey, Cowboy, come out wearing your guitar."

While the paint crew worked behind them, Tori and Cowboy stood on stage and went through their number. Cowboy played and sang a song from the show about shoppers entering a store through a revolving door. Each verse told of a different person, first a woman entering with several small children in tow, then a man carrying an oversized briefcase that catches in the door, then a woman finding herself pushed into the same space as a man with a cigar, and so on through a list of comic situations.

As Cowboy sang, Tori circled around him, using him as the centerpost of the revolving door.

She pantomimed each character that the song described. Several times Tori heard bursts of laughter from the students in the back of the auditorium working on the lighting system, or from the others painting on stage. It was hard not to smile back at them. Yet, in another way, their laughter made the practice easier because it reassured her that her efforts at comic pantomime were succeeding.

"Your facial expressions are good, Tori," Mrs. O said. "But you need to work on remembering that you are enclosed in a wedge of glass. Make the audience see that. Put up a hand or elbow to push the glass. Good. Swing your hip, turn suddenly to make the step in or out of the door. Try it this way."

The coach stood in the aisle below the stage, demonstrating movements. Tori watched carefully, then copied the motions, then refined them, adding her own comic touches. When Mrs. Odell called an end to their rehearsal, Tori glanced at her watch and was amazed to see that an hour had flown by. It had seemed only minutes.

Mrs. Odell said, "It's coming along well. We'll run over this number again next week. Till then, Cowboy, you work on slowing the tempo between the verse and refrain to give Tori time to circle you and switch to her next character. Tori, you practice in front of a full-length mirror."

"Right," Tori said.

"I rather like the green paint in your hair, but I don't suppose you'd care to leave it in for the play," Mrs. Odell added lightly, as she turned to walk away.

Tori clamped a hand to her head and shouted, "I forgot! How do I get this out?"

Cowboy said pleasantly, "Shave your head."

Tori howled in protest.

Looking up from the flat she was painting yellow, Shirl said, "This paint is water-soluble. It'll come out with shampoo."

At home that evening, Tori washed her hair, then positioned herself in front of her full-length mirror to practice her pantomime routine. As she worked on raising a shoulder, posing an arm, and defining the imaginary limits of the swinging door through her body gyrations, she chanted the words of Cowboy's song under her breath to match the timing.

"Life is a revolving door,
It spits one out and grabs one more — "

A quick toss of her head sent the wrapped towel on her hair sliding down over her face. She yelped, pushed it back, and began again. "Life is a — "

The phone rang.

"I'll get it!" Tori shouted, and dashed into the hall. "Hello?"

"Hello, is — Tori?"

It was Dom. She knew his voice. Tori hesitated, unsure if she should say his name. Would he think she had been waiting for him to phone? Worse, he might think that no other boys ever called her, and that was why she recognized his voice. She said, "This is Tori."

"I thought so. Hey, if you're busy I can call later."

So he was assuming that she had recognized

his voice. What would Shirl do now? Trying to sound casual, Tori said, "Who is this?"

"It's me. Dom."

His tone didn't give her any idea of his thoughts. He didn't sound surprised by her question, as though he had been sure she knew. Neither did he apologize for not identifying himself.

"Hi, Dom. Having trouble with math?"

"Yeah, but if you're busy — "

"Unh-uh. Wait a sec. I'll get my book." Tori ran to her room to collect her school papers. Why did she feel so tongue-tied? She always had an answer for everything and everyone. Why now, when Dom called, did her mind go blank? There must be some witty, clever thing she could say to him that would make him think she often chatted on the phone with boys. Or did he know that she'd never had a boyfriend? Tori knew that Dom had no steady girlfriend, Shirl had told her that, but no one knew whether Dom occasionally dated. Did boys ask each other the same questions about girls?

Returning to the phone, Tori said, "Okay, page eighty-seven, right?"

"Uh-huh. Third problem. I can't get it. Not a clue."

Leaning against the hallway door frame, Tori bent one knee up to form a ledge and opened her notebook on it. Since she had completed her homework before Dom phoned, she read off the steps she had used to solve the problem. "Is that how you did it?"

He said, "No. I didn't do anything. Didn't know where to start."

"Do you understand now?"

"I guess so."

A long silence hung between them while Tori tried desperately to think of something to say. Then Dom said, "Uh — thanks. Hope I didn't bother you."

"Oh no! I — hey, I was washing paint out of my hair."

"Paint? In your hair? How'd you do that?"

"Painting flats at school."

"Flats? What's that?"

"The things on stage, you know, they're wood frames with canvas on them. We paint the scenery on them."

"Oh."

Tori closed her notebook. With her back against the wall, she slid slowly downward until she sat on the floor. "Haven't you ever worked backstage?"

"On a play? I — I don't like that stuff. It's like giving speeches. I could never get up on a stage."

"You don't have to act in the play. You can work on the stage crew."

"Never thought about it," Dom said.

"It's a lot of fun. We paint flats and work on the riggings and set up lights."

"What are riggings?"

Tori explained, "Some flats lift up into the space above the stage. They're on lines and pulleys."

"I know how pulleys work," Dom said.

"You do? That makes you twice as smart as most of our crew."

Chapter 2

"Does Cowboy work on scenery?"

"No way! Once we tried to teach him how to build a set, but he hit his thumb more than he hit the nails. Then he ran around shouting that we had destroyed his career by damaging his precious hands."

"He's good on guitar."

"True," Tori admitted. "Look — uh — why not come backstage tomorrow? We could use help. I mean — if you have time and — if you'd like to."

Tori listened to her mouth blurt out words that she had never thought of saying to Dom. Her heartbeat quickened and she felt an odd tightening in her chest, as though she couldn't breathe.

Worse, Dom didn't answer. In the long silence Tori stared at her blue-jeaned legs propped up against the wall. Had she said too much? Did she sound pushy, asking him to join the stage crew? She would have asked any other boy; in fact, she often recruited other students to work on school activities. Somehow with Dom it was all different. She strained to keep her voice light. "It — it was just an idea. You're probably not interested."

He said finally, "I dunno. I've never — well, it might be okay. I'm pretty good with a hammer."

"Anybody who can use a hammer is welcome!" Relieved, Tori heard her enthusiasm flow into her own voice. "We've got the biggest pool of non-talent you ever saw! When they start letting me paint scenery, you know they're desperate. Would you believe I flunked art in kindergarten?"

"I'm pretty good at art. A lot better than at math."

"You're hired!"

Dom laughed, a low, quiet laugh that somehow matched his smile, filling Tori's mind with the image of his strong-boned face framed in waves of light hair.

He said, "See you tomorrow," and hung up.

Tori sat on the floor holding the phone receiver to her ear for several minutes after that final click, listening to the dial tone, not wanting to give up too quickly the memory of his voice. What exactly had he said? That he liked art, that he knew about pulleys, that he could use a hammer. She remembered a mention of Cowboy and a comment about not wanting to act.

Had he said he would work on the stage crew? Or had he only asked about it as he might ask about anything, curious to learn more, or maybe even only filling space with questions because he couldn't think of anything else to talk about? And even if he did think tonight that he might work backstage, how would he feel about it tomorrow? Should she have come right out and said, "Will you do it?" No, for once she was glad her tongue hadn't rushed off on its own. If he had been anyone else, she would have pressured him because the drama club always needed help. But he wasn't anyone else, he was Dom, and for reasons Tori wouldn't want to try to explain to anyone, he was special.

Did he think she was special? Probably not. Probably he only thought of her as a good math student. "Yuk," Tori muttered as she unwound herself from the phone cord. "Boys are the pits."

Chapter 3

Tori and Shirl sat cross-legged on the dusty stage in their paint-stained jeans and shirts. They were sitting behind the heavy, dark, stage curtains, which were pulled halfway open. They could see out to the apron of the stage, the area in front of the curtain line that curved toward the auditorium. Cowboy stood at its edge, rehearsing a scene with Eileen, the tall brunette who had the lead role in the play.

"She's so pretty," Shirl whispered.

"Yeah, if you like top-heavy," Tori whispered back.

Shirl giggled. "She has a nice shape."

Tori muttered, "I have a nice shape. You have a nice shape. Eileen does not have a nice shape, she has a sexy shape."

"Are you saying that *sexy* and *nice* aren't the same?" Shirl asked.

"How should I know? You're the one with the boyfriend."

Shirl reached out and hit Tori lightly on the knee with her clenched fist. Tori let out a mock shriek of pain. At the sound, Eileen swung around, glaring at both of them. The student director, who was taking Mrs. Odell's place for the afternoon, rapped with a pencil on a chair edge and asked for quiet.

"Hey, Tori, look who showed up," Shirl whispered.

Squinting into the half-darkened house area, Tori saw Dom slip into the back row of seats and settle quietly. With his attention focused on the acting, he did not see her.

Shirl whispered, "Tell me, girl with the new boyfriend, are *sexy* and *nice* the same?"

"He's here to help with sets, not to see me," Tori shrugged.

"If all he wanted to do was build sets, why didn't he show up the first week of school when we ran all those bulletin announcements asking people to turn out for stage crew?"

"Quiet, please," Tori whispered, raising her eyebrows and pulling down the corners of her mouth in imitation of the student director, but she was not looking at Shirl. She peered into the shadows, watching Dom, afraid he would leave. Although she could not see him clearly, she could imagine him watching the rehearsal with that same intent expression he sometimes wore when she glanced back at him in civics class, and he was watching Mr. Brown.

After Cowboy and Eileen finished their scene, Shirl flipped on all the overhead lights while Tori pulled the curtains open to the full width of the stage. Eileen walked majestically down the stage stairs, head high and shoulders back, to leave the auditorium, while Cowboy picked up a broom and remained on the stage. He swished it widely at the piles of wood shavings, nails, tacks, and torn bits of canvas that littered the floor.

"Watch out for the paint cans," Shirl said.

"Aw, Shirl. Come on, I can do a few things right," Cowboy said.

Shirl smiled. "Maybe one or two," she teased.

"Want to tell us what they are?" Tori asked, and Shirl made a face at her.

Tori's glance slid past Cowboy to watch Dom walk slowly up the aisle. He seemed to be hanging back, his hands pushed into his pockets, his head bowed slightly forward so that the lights shimmered on his hair. He stopped at the bottom of the stairs and his forehead creased in a slight frown, as though he were trying to make up his mind about something.

"You going to help or not?" Tori demanded. The words popped out, surprising them both.

Dom looked up, his eyes reflecting the stage lights. "What should I do?"

Tori glanced around, saw Shirl trying to paint over her head, and said, "For starters, you could get a ladder and do the top of Shirl's canvas."

Shirl said, "Oh, no, you'll get paint on your clothes. Anyway, I can get on the ladder."

"No, you can't," Tori said in such a firm voice that Dom raised his eyebrows, startled. Now that she'd spoken, she didn't know what to say next. Tori had no intention of explaining to him that Shirl wasn't supposed to climb ladders because of her back.

To her relief, Shirl smiled and said, "This needs to dry a while, anyway. Maybe you can paint tomorrow when you bring some paint clothes, Dom. Why don't you help Tori? She's supposed to be nailing together that mantel."

"That's right, auction him off to the highest bidder," Cowboy said as he wandered by carrying an armload of costumes.

Tori thought Dom's face reddened. But she wasn't sure because the stage lights were so bright. She said quickly, "Maybe you'd rather just watch for a while and see what we're doing."

She didn't want him to think that she had asked him to work on the stage crew so that she could get to know him better, or whatever other idea he might have. What would he think? With Cowboy around to make wisecracks, he might think anything.

As Dom rolled up his sleeves, he climbed the stairs toward her. "I'm pretty good with a hammer."

Tori led him over to the corner of the stage where she had started to assemble the false front for the scenery fireplace. When she touched the boards, to explain it to him, the whole piece swayed.

He said solemnly, "I think Shirl's right. You need help."

Tori punched him lightly on the shoulder. "That's not what you're supposed to say."

"No?"

"No. You're supposed to say that you think I am doing a wonderful job, but you'll be glad to help, even though anyone can see that I don't need help."

Dom smiled but didn't reply. Did he resent her punching him? Tori wondered. She and Cowboy and Shirl jabbed each other often when they were kidding around. She had done it without thinking. Now she felt shy, afraid he would think she was rude and pushy.

Other crew members wandered around them, carrying boards and canvas and tools, pounding together supports, adjusting riggings, and constructing a staircase to be used as part of the set. Dom's work on the fireplace won everyone's approval. By the end of the afternoon, Dom was considered a valuable member of the crew.

"Now that we know how clever you are, you'll be drafted for every production," Tori told him as they put away their tools in the storeroom behind the stage.

"That's okay," he said.

Cowboy poked his head through the doorway. "Want a ride home?"

"Right, be there in a sec," Tori said.

"How about you, Dom? Need a ride?"

"That's okay. I can walk."

"Of course you can walk. We can all walk. But what for, when Cowboy's got his car?" Tori asked.

"I gotta take Shirl and Tori for shakes. Don't leave me alone with the both of them," Cowboy said.

Tori started to say something more, then stopped, wondering if Shirl had told Cowboy to ask Dom. She bent over the brush she was washing, hoping Dom would think that it didn't matter to her whether he came with them.

He said to Cowboy, "Yeah, sure, I'll go with you."

Outside the pale sun hung low in the winter sky, sending yellow streaks of fading light through the gray clouds. Tori pulled her scarf out of the pocket of her ski parka and wrapped it around her neck. The four of them hurried across the parking lot to Cowboy's car. Tori and Shirl jumped up and down, and Dom rubbed his hands together briskly while they waited for Cowboy to dig his keys out of his pockets and unlock the doors.

"Think it'll snow tonight?" Shirl asked.

"Naw, it's not that cold," Cowboy said.

"It will be by the time you get your car open," Tori said.

"I'm hurrying! There, get in and shut up." Cowboy yanked open the door, pulled the front seat forward, and waited for Tori and Dom to climb in the backseat. Tori settled into the far corner and wrapped her scarf's fringed ends around her hands. Dom's long legs seemed to fill the space between the front and back seats.

"You have enough room?" Tori asked.

"I'm fine."

"You look like a pretzel," Tori said. "Cowboy, it's freezing. Does that heater work?"

As he started the car, Cowboy said, "You're in for a big thrill, honey chile. I got it fixed yesterday."

They drove out of the parking lot, past the flat-roofed brick school buildings with their covered walkways, past the football field, and through the surrounding residential area until they reached the edge of the business district. The drive-in hamburger place was a round, glass-walled building with its roof painted red and white to resemble a circus tent. Cowboy rolled down his window to order shakes and fries from a carhop dressed in a clown suit.

When Tori recognized the carhop as a boy in her history class, she leaned across Dom to shout, "Hey, your taste in clothes is definitely improving!"

Cowboy laughed.

The boy glared at Tori and muttered, "Drop dead, Baniff," before he hurried away.

Tori shrugged. "Some people just can't handle compliments."

Shirl said, "That's rough to have to wear that weird costume. I don't think I'd take the job."

Dom said, "Finding a job is rough."

After their order came, Cowboy closed the window and kept the heater running. Tori's hands felt numb from holding the cold milkshake in its tall paper container. They passed the catsup back and forth with the fries. She could barely feel the oil and salt on her cold fingers, but the odor of fries filled the car.

Dom asked, "How's your part in the play going?"

"It's not much. You'll have to look fast to see me. Cowboy and I have a song together."

"That's the best part of the show," Shirl said.

Cowboy said, "You better believe it, little lady! We're gonna knock 'em dead."

"You'll love the play, Dom," Shirl said.

"I enjoyed the scene I saw today."

Cowboy let out a hoot. "Eileen, you mean! She's something to watch!"

"Yeah, if Barbie dolls turn you on," Tori said.

Shirl and Cowboy laughed but Dom frowned. Something in his expression made Tori uncomfortable, yet she couldn't sort out what. It was possible that Dom was a friend of Eileen's, and that he thought Tori had meant her remark as an insult. Or more likely, he didn't know that Barbie dolls were plastic dolls with deadpan faces and grotesquely exaggerated figures. As there was no way to guess his feelings, Tori glanced around, looking for a quick change of subject. When Cowboy licked salt from his fingers, Tori said, "Gross, Cowboy, gross."

"Would it be better if I wiped my hands on your sleeve?" he asked and reached across the back seat toward her.

Shrinking away from him, Tori shrieked. Then she grabbed up the handful of paper napkins that she had saved from the tray and tossed them at Cowboy. They fluttered down past his outstretched hand to the floor beneath Dom's legs.

Dom leaned forward, picked them up, and neatly piled them back on the seat beside Tori. His hand brushed hers. Had he meant to touch her? she wondered.

"C'mon, let's go, I'm late for supper," Cowboy said.

"After gorging on all this neat junk food?" Tori demanded. "That's even more gross!"

"One more crack out of you, Baniff, and you walk home," Cowboy said.

Chapter 3

Laughing, Tori said, "I take it back. You're my idol, you gorgeous hunk, you."

When they drove home, Cowboy stopped at Tori's house first. Shirl slid forward pulling the seat toward her to let Tori out. Tori closed the car door and then turned to lean in through the window. "Thanks for the ride, idol. See you tomorrow, Shirl. You, too, Dom."

As she hurried up the walk toward her house, she realized that she didn't know whether or not Cowboy or Shirl had answered her. She only remembered Dom's smile. His blue eyes shone as they reflected the fading daylight.

He had said softly, "Thanks, Tori. See you tomorrow."

Tori bounced up the three steps to the front door, turned, and stood peering through the twilight at the empty street, imagining the car still there, imagining Dom saying, "Thanks, Tori. See you tomorrow."

Why had he thanked her? She searched her memory for a reason but could find nothing. The crisp air chilled her face. She could smell the cold, a clear, tangy smell of swirling winds and frozen puddles and decaying leaves beneath hedges. With so much winter all around her, she could not explain why she felt such a warm glow rising inside her. It was foolishness, she knew, the sort of thing her mother's friends liked to laugh about and call "puppy love" or some other dumb name. They were wrong. She didn't imagine herself in love. She knew that she didn't know Dom well enough to love him. Nonetheless, there was something about the way his face shone when he smiled that made her feel uncomfortable and happy at the same time.

Behind her the door swung open. Her father peered out, saying, "I thought I heard a car drive up. What are you doing, just standing there? Supper's ready."

Tori followed him into the hall. "Sorry I'm late."

"I don't know about all this play practice. Are you sure you're doing your schoolwork?" He stopped to peer at her over the top of his reading glasses.

Tori giggled. "You look about a hundred years old when you do that."

"Never mind the jokes. What about your grades?"

"Now, Dad, would you rather have an honor student for a daughter or a world-famous actress?"

"An honor student."

"Oh, you! You sound just like a parent!"

"A hungry parent," he corrected her. "Hurry up, now."

Chapter 4

"Sometimes I feel like the storeroom is my home-away-from-home," Tori told Dom as they stood at the sink washing out the brushes. "I spend more time here than anyplace else."

He said, "That's because the rest of the crew just toss their stuff through the door and run. You stay behind to pick up and straighten out the shelves."

"That's me, Cinderella."

The storeroom was located at the end of a short corridor past the dressing rooms. It was the size of a walk-in closet, with shelves lining both sides and a small sink in a Formica counter wedged on the end wall beneath a window. Carelessly stacked boxes filled with old costumes, paint equipment, and stage props such as dishes, tablecloths, mirrors, umbrellas, and telephones filled the shelves. Most of the props were discards donated by parents or collected by students.

Cowboy tossed a cane and a fireman's hat in the direction of the doorway. They clattered to the floor.

Tori shouted, "You come back and pick that up!"

Drying his hands on the rag above the sink, Dom said, "I'll get it."

While Dom picked up and put away a stack of items left by other students, Cowboy poked his head back in through the doorway. "Ready to go, you two?"

"Thanks — uh — I have a car," Dom said. "Uh — I can take Tori home. That is, unless you want to go now, Tori?"

Tori stared down at her hands in the soapy water. She wished she knew whether Dom had offered to take her home simply to be polite, even though he didn't particularly want to offer a ride, or because he wanted to be alone with her.

Over her shoulder she said, "I'm not done here. You go ahead, Cowboy."

"Yeah, well, keep the door open, you two," Cowboy said, and left.

"I'll shut it with your head in it if you don't get out of here," Tori shouted after him. Cowboy's laughter echoed in the hall.

Tori hung the brushes on their drying rack above the sink, rinsed off the counter, then turned to find Dom still kneeling on the floor, repacking messy boxes.

"You don't need to straighten up this whole room," Tori said.

He smiled up at her. "I don't mind."

"Hey, I don't want you to think I suggested you help on the stage crew as a trick to get you on cleanup."

"I don't think that."

"I — we — really do need people who can do carpentry."

Chapter 4

"Yes," Dom said, and the corners of his mouth twitched, as though he was holding back laughter.

"That's obvious, huh?"

"There's a lot of good acting talent," Dom said.

Tori laughed. "Everybody wants to be a star, get their name in the paper, and all that stuff. Nobody wants to work behind the scenes, where there's no glory."

"I guess that's so whether you're talking about plays or sports," Dom said.

"It's probably even true with the paper. Everybody wants to write articles and get by-lines, but nobody wants to sell ads."

"I can understand that better," Dom said.

"You can? Why?"

"I — uh — selling ads, that's kind of like being onstage. Or giving speeches in front of class."

"What's wrong with giving speeches? I like speech class."

"I guess you would."

"What classes do you like?" Tori asked.

"Oh, things like art and shop, where I can work with my hands. And I like history and science. I kind of like Spanish, the reading part, but not the conversation."

"I never can understand what the teacher says when she speaks Spanish."

"I can understand, all right," Dom said. "But I can't think of anything to answer."

Tori leaned back against the sink and stared at him, surprised at the idea that was slowly filling her mind. She had known lots of girls who were so shy that they had trouble talking to other people, but she never thought boys were that shy —

at least, not tall, handsome boys. They all walked with such long, easy gaits, their arms swinging with the rhythmic turning of their broad shoulders, their heads high. She said, "Anyhow, I'm glad you wanted to help us."

He closed the box, stood up, and slid it in place on the shelf. Smiling down at her, he said, "Me, too. Ready to leave?"

"My coat's in my locker," she said, closing up the storeroom.

In the main corridor the janitors had turned off the overhead lights, leaving the security lights shining above the exit doors. The narrow bank of lockers in the center of the hall cast deep shadows. Tori pulled her parka from her locker and started to struggle into it. Dom caught the collar and held it for her. When he settled the jacket across her shoulders, his fingers touched the back of her neck. She pretended not to notice.

When they climbed into Dom's car, he asked, "You want to stop at the drive-in?"

"What time is it?"

"Six-fifteen."

"Oh, damn, I'm already late for supper. Mom doesn't care, but Dad goes through the roof."

As they drove through the darkening streets, Tori glanced at Dom. He kept his eyes on the road, his hands clenched on the wheel.

"This is your car?" she asked. It didn't look new enough to be his parents' car, but it wasn't a heap.

"No, it's my brother's. He's at college."

"How come he didn't take his car?"

Chapter 4

Dom patted the dashboard. "Nellie'd never make it nine hundred miles."

"Is that what you call the car? Nellie?"

"That's what my brother calls it."

"I didn't know you had a brother." Tori held up her scarf end in front of her face as though it were a portable microphone, speaking into it in the clipped enunciation of a TV newscaster. "Come right down to it, I do not have enough information for my in-depth report, Mr. Hallett. If you would just answer a few questions for our viewers — let's see — I am sure all the folks out there in TV land would like to know how many members there are in your family, how you first happened to choose the theater as a profession, and how you feel now that you have won the Emmy for nail-pounding."

Dom eased the car up to the curb in front of Tori's house, turned off the engine, then faced her. He hooked his elbow over the back seat so that his hand dangled inches from Tori's shoulder. Although he seemed unaware of it, Tori could feel his nearness as keenly as if he was a bonfire.

He said, "I have two brothers, one younger, one older, no sisters, two parents, and a cocker spaniel."

"A real honest-to-gosh cocker spaniel?" Tori said into her scarf-mike. "Incredible, Mr. Hallett. No doubt it is from this family member that you draw your artistic inspiration."

"She's only part cocker spaniel."

"Ah, mixed media! My audience will be thrilled."

Dom grinned and said, "Tori, you're crazy."

"I am also late for dinner," Tori said, as she reached behind herself and opened the car door. "Thanks for the ride."

"Yeah, sure. Maybe I'll call you tonight. If you're going to be home."

"I'll be home. I'm always home on weeknights. My parents are right out of the ice age."

"Oh! Maybe I shouldn't phone."

Tori said quickly, "No, they don't mind phone calls. I didn't mean to make them sound like jailers. They're really nice, only they're really old-fashioned, too. I think they watch too much TV. They think that if kids are out of the house on weeknights, they end up in the clutches of drug pushers. Don't ask me to explain. They let me go out weekends. Maybe they think the pushers stay home on weekends."

"They probably think you should study on weeknights. Mine are the same way."

Tori raised her eyebrows in mock surprise. "Very perceptive, Dr. Watson."

Dom phoned that evening.

After that he always drove his car to school and gave Tori a ride home. He phoned each night. On Friday night he met her in the stands at the basketball game. They hadn't planned to meet. He had asked if she would be going to the game, and she had said yes, certain he would ask to meet her there, but he didn't. And she couldn't ask him.

As she told Shirl, "I wish I knew why boys ask questions like that. I mean, if you asked if I was going to the game, I'd say, 'Sure, what about you? Want to meet me there?' But I can't say that to a boy."

They were sitting in the stands above the court, crushed between a mass of arms and legs that were too long for the narrow width between bleacher rows. The gym ceiling lights reflected off the glossy surface of the floor. The gym had its own peculiar odor of varnish and overheated bodies, which lingered whether the room was full or empty.

"He must like you, Tori. He wouldn't drive you home every day if he didn't like you."

"Maybe. Or maybe he's got nothing else to do."

"I don't believe that."

Tori's parents had dropped her off at the game on their way to a party. Knowing that Shirl and Cowboy would be at the game, Tori was sure of a ride home. As she watched the players race down the floor, ducking between their opponents, her mind drifted back to the storeroom behind the stage. That's where Dom had asked if she were going to the game. She had thought he would say more, maybe offer to pick her up or say that he would meet her there, but after she had told him that she always went to the games, he had suddenly become very busy organizing the shelves. During the ride home he talked about math class. Or rather, he asked Tori a couple of questions, and she had done most of the talking. When she tried to remember what he had said, all she could recall were a few questions about math. He hadn't said anything personal.

"Hey, get that pass!" Cowboy shouted. "Did ya see that? Did ya see that?" He reached around Shirl and punched Tori's arm.

"Get your hands off my bod," Tori snapped.

Cowboy leaned forward to look at her, his red hair falling in his eyes. "What's with you, grouchy?"

Before Tori could reply, the crowd broke into screams of excitement, and Cowboy's attention returned to the game.

Shirl whispered, "There he is, Tori! I *knew* he'd show up."

Dom stood in the doorway of the gym, his glance sweeping the stands, then the floor. He watched the action. Tori watched him. He was relaxed, his hands in his pockets, his eyes wide and alert. His light hair waved back from his face.

"Stand up so he'll see you," Shirl said.

"Oh, terrific! Maybe I should have brought pom-poms. What makes you think he's looking for me?"

"What makes you think he isn't?"

Tori pressed a clenched fist against her mouth. "I don't know, Shirl. How can I tell?"

Shirl squeezed Tori's arm but said nothing. Tori sat in agony, trying not to stare at Dom but unable to keep her attention on the game. With so many people in the gym, how would he ever see her, even if he wanted to? And if he did want to, why hadn't he told her he would be coming to the game? He could have said anything, something like "Save a seat for me," but he hadn't. Probably he didn't want to see her. Maybe he was looking for someone else. Maybe he had another girlfriend that Shirl didn't know about, a girl who went to another high school.

He looked up and his eyes met Tori's. With a grin and a wave, he headed toward her, climbing up the bleachers through the confusion of people.

Before she could think what to say, he loomed over her, asking, "Any room here?"

"Shove over," Shirl said to Cowboy, and somehow they made room for him between Shirl and Tori.

"How's the game going?" He settled himself into place, pressing against Tori. Now all she could think of was Dom's warmth radiating through his T-shirt and jeans. His legs were folded up in the narrow space between the rows, his jacket wedged between his knees. When he leaned forward to watch the game, his bare arm touched hers.

As she had no idea how the game was going, Tori checked the scoreboard, then said, "Incredible! We're not losing!"

They chatted about the game, discussing plays and comparing their own basketball skills, while Tori's thoughts kept skipping off in other directions. When Dom wasn't looking at her, she tried not to stare at him, but found it impossible. It was as though she were taking inventory, memorizing the faded-tan brown of his arm with its glow of blond hairs, the thickness of his wrist, the way his fingertips squared, the worn jean cloth over his raised knee. Would he ask to take her home? Would he stand at the end of the game, say goodbye, and then move away with the crowd? Would she be able to smile and say something nonchalant, to let him know that she didn't expect to go home with him, didn't even want to?

Then he turned, caught her watching him, and said, "I almost didn't get here. My mom needed my brother's car. I thumbed a ride with a neighbor."

Tori heard her old, self-confident self say, "We can give you a ride home, can't we, Cowboy?"

She had to lean forward and repeat the question twice before Cowboy heard her above the noise. Then Cowboy's eyes narrowed, he bared his crooked teeth in a leer, and said, "Only if you promise to keep your hands off my bod."

With a behave-yourself scowl at Cowboy, Shirl said, "Of course you can ride with us, Dom."

After the game they stopped by the drive-in for shakes, then headed for Tori's house. Cowboy flipped on his car radio, reached across the seat, and pulled Shirl close to him. Tori slid down in the seat, embarrassed, unsure how to act until she noticed that Dom was staring out the window on his side of the car. Did he feel as uncomfortable as she did? Tori quipped, "They've been married since they were five years old."

Dom leaned toward her, speaking below the sound level of the radio. "I'll have the car tomorrow night, Tori. You want to go somewhere?"

"Like where?"

"I dunno. I could take you to a movie."

"You could come over and watch TV if you want," Tori said, not knowing if he could afford to take her out. Shirl frequently paid for her own ticket when she went out with Cowboy, but Tori didn't think she knew Dom well enough to suggest that.

"I'd rather go out," he said, so she supposed that settled the question of what he could afford.

"*The Empire Strikes Back* is playing."

"You're a *Star Wars* fan? Great!"

"You, too?"

"I collect sci-fi movie posters," he said. "Listen, I'll pick you up at seven, okay?"

Cowboy parked in front of Tori's house, saying, "You can walk her up to the door and kiss her good night, son, but don't touch her bod." Then he let out a low groan that made Tori suspect that Shirl had socked him.

As Tori climbed out of the back seat, she tried to keep her voice light, despite an urge to shout out her anger. At least in the darkness no one could see the red flames that she could feel burning in her cheeks. "Thank you, big daddy, but I can manage my own love life without your guiding light. I can also find my front door all by myself, unlike some retarded redheads."

She held her mouth in a stiff grin and waved until the car pulled away, then stamped up the front steps. If Dom had even considered walking her to the front door, he couldn't possibly have done so after Cowboy's stupid remark. She stormed into the kitchen, ready to lash out at the next person she saw.

Her mother sat at the table, finishing a cup of coffee. "Have a nice evening, darling?"

"Rotten, rotten, rotten," Tori stormed. "That stupid Cowboy! You know what he said?"

"No."

"Honestly, sometimes I think he's demented. His brains are as crooked as his teeth!"

Her mother looked at her thoughtfully. "Cowboy can't help his teeth."

"He can sure help his brains!"

"Yes, but that's not the same. Criticize what he says or does, if you think he deserves criticism, but don't make fun of something he can't help."

Tori threw up her hands in disgust. "What is this? First Cowboy says something stupid, and then you bawl me out."

Her mother sighed, walked over to the sink, and poured out the rest of her coffee. "Sorry, sweetie. I had a rough day at work and then a long evening at a dull cocktail party, and my legs ache. I didn't mean to fuss at you. You want to tell me about your problem with Cowboy?"

Tori thought a minute. "No, it's not important. I — I'm sorry, Mom. Uh — Dom asked me to go to the movies tomorrow night."

"Dom? The boy who brings you home from school? That's nice."

Yes, it was nice. It balanced out her anger with Cowboy; in fact, in some ways, she wished she and Dom were going out with Cowboy and Shirl. Not that she wanted Cowboy along, but she would feel more comfortable with Shirl there. Did Dom know that she had never been out alone with another boy, or would he think from Cowboy's remark that she had dated lots of boys? Would he ask Cowboy? Even if he did ask Cowboy, he might get any sort of answer because Cowboy said whatever popped into his head, not what was actually so.

Chapter 4

Dom arrived at seven the next evening. He stood on the doorstep under the porch light, until Tori said, "Come on in and meet my parents."

Something in his face reminded her of the way she had felt in first grade when she was sent to the principal's office for talking back to her teacher. "It's okay, they don't bite," she said.

He grinned but still looked nervous. Tori introduced him, saying, "Mom, Dad, this is Dom Hallett. He's our newest, most useful stage crew member. In fact, if the set doesn't collapse in the middle of my routine, you can thank Dom, who knows how to drive a nail straight."

Her parents said, "Nice to meet you, Dom," and he smiled and mumbled, "Me, too."

It wasn't the most original answer, but Tori could tell from the way her parents nodded that they liked him.

Tori had thought she would be nervous, but she found that she was more at ease with him when they were alone than when they were with Cowboy and Shirl. In his car it was as though they were alone together in the storeroom, talking about the play and math class, keeping the conversation on subjects they could both handle.

Standing in line at the theater ticket booth, their hands shoved in their pockets, their breath making white clouds, they both watched the crowd and waved occasionally to friends.

"I hope this show is worth the wait," Dom said.

"I'd wait all night for Darth Vader."

"What about Han Solo?"

"Him I wouldn't cross the street for."

In the darkened theater they shared a box of popcorn, their fingers touching when they passed it to each other. Twice when Tori looked at Dom she found him staring at her, his eyes bright in the flickering light from the screen. Each time he turned quickly away.

As the tension built in a galactic chase scene, Dom whispered close to her ear, "Your hero is winning."

"Darth Vader? Yeah, but you know Hollywood. They'll double-cross him in the end."

"How come you like Darth Vader?"

"I always like the underdog."

"Some underdog," he whispered, then settled back in his seat to watch.

It wasn't until Dom parked the car in front of her house that Tori remembered this was a date, not just a ride home from school. They walked slowly toward her door, discussing the movie, but in the back of her mind she could hear Cowboy telling Dom that he could kiss her good night but not to touch her bod. Maybe Dom had forgotten. Cowboy made so many smart remarks, surely Dom wouldn't remember them all, especially not that one.

She said, "I'd love to be an astronaut, but I get seasick in a swing."

"I don't think that's a problem. I mean, there's no motion in a space ship."

"You sure about that?"

"Tell you what, if a space ship ever lands in my backyard, and the little green men take me for a ride, I'll let you know."

Chapter 4

"You mean you'd stand there and wait for them to grab you?"

"What would you do? Hide under your bed?"

"Yes." Tori peered up at him and was startled to find that he was so close to her that she could feel his breath on her forehead. They stared at each other in silence.

Finally Dom said, "Now what?"

"What do you mean, now what?"

"You tell me."

Tori shrugged. "You want to come in? We could search the fridge."

"No, it's late. I have to get home." But he didn't move. Instead he stood quietly, watching her.

Tori giggled. "You want me to walk you back to your car?"

"No."

"Then what do you want?"

A grin turned up the corners of his mouth. "Tell me what Cowboy meant last night."

"About what?"

"You know — about not touching you."

"You're asking me to explain what that moron says!" Tori shrieked, then clapped her hand over her mouth. In a whisper, she added, "I think my folks are asleep. I'd better go in."

"Right." He started down the stairs, then turned and said softly, "Hey, Tori."

"Uh-huh?"

He was standing on the step below her. Their faces were on a level. She felt his hand touch her hair. He leaned forward and kissed her mouth. Then he was gone.

Chapter 5

Tori's hand shook as she carefully underlined her eyebrows with the white stage makeup that was designed to catch the footlights. Her soft oval face, with its small nose and bright eyes, stared back at her from the poorly lit mirror in the boys' dressing room. Strands of hair fell from the loosened hair clips.

"I look awful," she wailed. "I have no bone structure. I look like a face painted on a balloon."

"Here, you're fine, turn around," Marge, the girl in charge of makeup, said. "You need some shadow on your cheeks to give you cheekbones. There, that's better. And a little color. And a streak of lightener to give your nose a little more length and shape. Now look."

Tori glared at her reflection. Marge's talented fingers had painted in shadows and highlights of makeup, giving Tori's face an illusion of slenderness, with a well-defined nose.

"Wow, I look like a person!"

Marge laughed. "Now go out and knock them dead!"

As Tori opened the dressing room door, she felt an odd sinking feeling in her chest, a wave of nausea that she could not recall having felt before. Stage fright? Was this what stage fright was? Everyone talked about it, but Tori had never before experienced it. She bit her lip and hurried toward the spot for her entrance. Glancing around for Dom, she met Shirl's smile.

"Is Dom here?" Tori whispered.

"Haven't seen him. He must be out front."

Tori groaned, her eyebrows drawing together in an expression of dismay. She would be terrible, she knew she would. She would miss her cue and probably forget her lines. And Dom would be in the audience watching.

From on stage she heard Eileen's high voice recite the speech that cued Tori's entrance and Eileen's exit. Cowboy slapped his guitar. The audience laughed.

With the sudden rush of sound, Tori relaxed and her reflexes took over, propelling her onto the stage in the skipping walk that she had practiced for so many hours both on stage and in front of her mirror at home.

"So there you are," Cowboy recited. The spotlight glittered off the sequin band that he had added to his old Stetson.

Tori shrugged, jutted out one hip, and made a face at him, a gesture that looked nonchalant and spontaneous because she had practiced the timing so carefully. The audience rewarded her with laughter.

And then there wasn't any audience. It was as though she were going through the routine for Mrs. O, with only Cowboy and the stage crew watching; completely confident, her voice clear, her gestures timed, her expressions outrageous. She sailed through the short dialogue with Cowboy, danced into her pantomime, acted out each character in the revolving door number, and skipped off the stage to a roar of applause.

"Go back and take a bow," Mrs. O whispered from the wings.

Tori skipped out, pulled a funny face, bowed, and turned to go offstage. She was waved back again and took three bows before the audience would quiet down and let the scene continue.

When she finally ran off the stage and down the hall to the dressing room, Shirl caught her in a hug. "You were marvelous! Oh, Tori, you stole the show!"

"Did I? Was I all right?" she gasped.

"All right! You were fantastic!"

Tori sighed with relief. "Oh, God, I was shaking all over."

"No one could have guessed."

"I was okay once I got onstage, but it was awful before that."

They tiptoed back to stand behind the curtains and watch the rest of the play. It went fairly smoothly, but Eileen seemed more nervous than she had in rehearsal. Her voice thinned to a high pitch, her gestures looked wooden. She recited stiffly, "Listen, dahling, you have saved my life. Without your absolute and overwhelming talent, I could not have gone on."

Marching across the stage to grab the bell pull, she continued, "I really cannot imagine where the butler is," but she slurred the word *butler* so that it sounded as though she had said *butter*.

Chapter 5

Unnerved, she yanked too hard on the bell pull. The velvet rope tore loose from the staples that held it to the flat and fell to the floor.

Eileen stared, horrified, then mumbled her next line. "And when you're rich and famous, you won't forget me, will you?"

A polite silence from the audience answered her as Cowboy stood, mouth open, staring, and missed his cue. A voice backstage whispered, "I could never . . ."

Cowboy recovered and said quickly, "I could never forget," which drew a muffled titter from the audience.

Their timing faltered. Cowboy missed another cue. The scene lagged. Suddenly he gave an odd shrug that was not in the script, ad-libbed a line that put the scene back on track, and picked up the tempo. By the time the curtain closed, the audience was laughing again, but not as much as earlier.

Behind the closed curtain, Cowboy spit out a few profanities. As the curtain parted, he glared with a frozen smile as the rest of the cast marched back onto the stage to join him and Eileen for the applause. The audience responded with polite enthusiasm but doubled their noise when Tori skipped out, stopped at Cowboy's side, and took a deep bow.

"Let's go get bombed," Cowboy muttered in her ear as she straightened up.

Tori kept her stage grin on her face until the final curtain. Then she asked, "Aren't you going to the cast party?"

"Yeah, sure, and drown my sorrows in fruit punch."

Stage crew members pushed around them, folding up the sets and carrying off the props. Tori hurried back to the dressing room to change into her jeans and sweater. The small room was filled with girls, shouting, and piles of dumped costumes. By the time she had rubbed most of the makeup from her face, the boys were banging on the door for their turn to use the room. Tori spread her elbows and shoved her way through them, clearing a path for Shirl to follow her into the corridor.

Dom caught her arm, pulling her free of the crowd. "You were great," he said, his face shining in a way that made Tori's heart beat faster.

"Were you out front?"

"Yeah, I wanted to see you. I was afraid that if I stayed backstage, I'd miss something."

"You going to the party?"

"Sure I am. I'll be late, though. I want to help knock down the flats and get stuff stored away."

Cowboy shouted from across the crowd, "Come on, Baniff, we're leaving!"

"I'll stay and help," Tori told Dom.

He said, "No, you go ahead."

"You don't trust me. You think I'll break stuff," she teased.

"I've seen you with a hammer. We're safer without you."

"Some friend you are!"

Cowboy shouted, "Move it!"

Dom's fingers tightened where he still held her arm, then dropped away. Smiling, he said, "Go on, Tori. A star can't do cleanup. I'll be over as soon as we finish here."

He left her and headed for the stage. Although Tori would have liked to wait for Dom, she joined Cowboy and Shirl. If she stayed behind now, Dom might think she was acting as though she owned him. Caught up in the babble of voices and people, Tori piled into the nearest car.

Because Marge had a large family room in her basement, they held the cast party there. Her parents had draped crepe paper streamers from doorways and windowsills to the ceiling to form a colorful canopy. The stereo blared. The soft drink cans dripped ice water. People surrounded Tori, shouted compliments at her, then did imitations of some of her pantomime gestures.

She felt Shirl slip an arm around her shoulders. Cowboy patted her head.

"I'm not your pet pup," she shouted at him above the roar.

"Can't touch your bod, can't touch your head," he teased.

Tori held out a limp-wristed hand, saying, "Okay, you can hold my hand."

Instead, Cowboy grabbed her arm and held up her hand as though she were a prizefighter in a ring.

"The winnah!" he shouted. "You saved the show!"

Tori shouted back, "You were the star! You were terrific!"

He dropped her hand. "Yeah, if you forget the last scene."

Tori stretched to her full height, shoved out

her chest until she could arch her back no further, held her head at a haughty angle, and in a perfect imitation of Eileen's high, strained pitch in the last scene, she said: "Listen, dahling, you saved my life! Without your absolute, immeasurable, and overwhelming talent, I cannot see how we could have gone on."

Around them, everyone giggled.

"I should have been quite dead without you to save me," Tori continued, her voice rising. "But worse than death, without you I could never have found the butter!"

Shirl whispered, "Tori, stop."

Beyond the sea of faces, Tori caught a glimpse of Eileen.

Eileen stood frozen, her eyes wide, her face pale. For a brief moment Tori felt panic, but then Cowboy applauded, shouting, "It's in the fridge behind the eggs you laid!"

Others crowded around them, blocking out Eileen. Tori forgot her. In a high, theatrical voice she ad-libbed, "And when they place that rhinestone crown on you, don't forget me, dahling. I'll be the egg in the background singing, 'There he goes, Mr. America!' "

Cowboy did a clumsy pirouette. Tori caught his hand, saying, "No, no, dahling, you must practice your runway walk. Let an expert teach you."

With her head still high, chest out, she did a slow, hip-swinging walk in front of him. Cowboy followed with mincing steps, imitating her sway until they were both laughing so hard that they had to stop. By then they had the attention of everyone at the party. The applause and cheers drowned out the stereo.

Someone shouted, "Come on, do your number from the show, Tori."

Before she could think about it, Cowboy had his guitar out. He strummed the chorus, then began his song. "Life is a revolving door — "

While everyone clapped in time, Tori danced around him, doing her pantomime. The crowd picked up the chorus words, then the verses, and sang them over and over, keeping Tori dancing. Finally, exhausted, she stopped, threw up her hands and said, "Play something else before I drop dead!"

Warm, perspiring, and thirsty, Tori edged her way through the singing, swaying cast members, searching for the ice chest of canned drinks. As the stereo blared disco, bodies twisted and arms shot out. When she neared the refreshment table, Tori saw Dom standing at the bottom of the basement stairs, his back to her. She worked her way toward him until she stood behind him, then started to reach out to touch his arm.

She heard him say, "You were great, Eileen."

Past his shoulder she saw Eileen, her coat over her arm, her hand on the banister. "Thanks. Well, good night."

"Can't — uh — can't you stay a while?"

"No, my head is splitting and it's so hot and noisy in here."

"Yeah, well, listen, you need a ride home?"

Eileen's lower lip quivered. She said quickly, "You're nice, Dom. No thanks, I have a car."

To Tori's amazement Eileen bit her lip as though she were fighting back tears, then ran up the stairs.

Tori said, "What's wrong with her?"

Dom said, "Hi, Tori." He didn't smile, but he didn't frown, either. He dug his hands in his pockets and stared around the room.

Tori caught his elbow. "You just get here? Got some great junk food. Let's go pig out."

As they wandered past the refreshment table, sampling cold drinks, chips, nuts, cookies, brownies, Tori said, "Get all the sets down?"

"Sure."

"How much did you break?"

"Without you, we did great."

"Thanks, friend. You're what my ego needs."

"Since when does your ego need anything?" he said. He didn't look at her when he said it.

"What's that supposed to mean?" she demanded.

Dom shrugged but didn't answer. As the music from the stereo switched to a slow number and someone dimmed the lights, he held out his hands and drew Tori into his arms, leading her into the middle of the crowd of swaying couples. Tori's back stiffened and her mind went blank. She tried to think of something clever to say, but instead she found herself wondering if her breath smelled of potato chips.

Dom's chin pressed against the side of her forehead, his shoulder blocked her vision, and his arm held her tightly, so that Tori's only contact with the rest of the party was through the sounds around her and the occasional bumping of other couples. As Dom's grip tightened, she relaxed, closed her eyes, and let her face rest against his shoulder, but her thoughts continued to swirl. She had heard him offer to give Eileen a ride. What if Eileen had accepted? Did he mean only to take Eileen home and then return to the party? Or had he planned to spend the rest of the evening with her? Was it Eileen he really wished he were holding in his arms? How was Tori supposed to compete with anyone as pretty as that?

For a few minutes, while she was doing her number with Cowboy, she had felt like the star of the party, but now, remembering Dom's offer to Eileen, she snapped back to reality. Tori knew that although she was cute onstage, offstage she was plain Victoria Baniff, typical Miss Average.

Cowboy muttered in her ear, "Break it up, lovers."

Tori jerked her head back and glared at Cowboy. He swayed slowly, holding Shirl close to him, his freckled face resting on the top of her blonde head.

Tori said, "Look who's preaching."

Cowboy dropped one eyelid in a slow wink. "You two need a ride tonight?"

Tori wished she could reach out and kick Cowboy. How could he say anything so stupid? What did he mean, "You two"? Dom hadn't said he would take her home after the party. Certainly she had hoped he would, but that wasn't the same thing as being asked.

Then Dom said, "Thanks, but we've got a car."

Chapter 6

Tori sat cross-legged on her bed, hunched over the phone. Into the receiver she said, "I dunno, Shirl. I'm so mixed up."

"He did take you home, didn't he?" Shirl's calm voice replied. "Why would he do that if he didn't like you?"

Tori snapped, "How could he get out of it? Cowboy cornered him."

"He didn't mean to. You know Cowboy. He thought he was being nice, offering a ride."

"Yeah, I know. I'm not mad at Cowboy. It's just — Shirl, Dom was, well, you know, like we had something going. Anyhow, until last night. I mean, he was polite last night, too damn polite. Like he was trying to tell me off. And then there's that other thing. About Eileen. I heard him ask to take her home. So it was like, after she left, he was stuck with me."

There was a short silence. Then Shirl said, "I don't think Dom really wanted to take Eileen home."

"So why did he ask her?"

"I think he felt sorry for her."

"Why? Because she blew a few lines in the

play?" But even as she asked it, Tori knew that wasn't why.

"Umm. Maybe."

"Maybe nothing! He was embarrassed! By me! He was, wasn't he, Shirl? He was embarrassed because I did that dumb imitation of Eileen," Tori groaned.

"Well, it was funny, only — well, sometimes you don't think. I mean, you do imitations to be funny but, well, it isn't so funny for the person you're imitating."

"I don't hurt people on purpose, Shirl!"

"I know you don't, hon," Shirl said softly.

"I just open my mouth, and it's three days later before I know what I've said!"

Shirl giggled. "Don't worry. It'll be okay. If you want, Cowboy could ask Dom to double-date with us. That would kind of get things going again."

Tori wailed, "Don't do that! I can't force Dom to like me. Oh, Shirl! If only I were like you! Nobody ever gets mad at you."

After hanging up the phone, Tori glared at her reflection in the full-length mirror on the back of her closet door. Jutting out a hip, she pulled a funny face. Then she stuck out her tongue at her reflection. If only she could remain serious and look frail and feminine like Shirl, or voluptuous and feminine like Sonja and Eileen, then she would be the kind of girl Dom really wanted, she thought. Shoving her fingers through her unruly hair, she tried to flatten it around her face into a sleek, sophisticated style. When Marge had made Tori up for the play, Tori's face had almost looked glamorous. Maybe — maybe — Tori turned her face sideways and peered from the corners of her eyes at her three-quarter reflection. Maybe if she looked sleek and sophisticated, she could act that way.

She still had the money that her grandmother and Aunt Ruth had sent her for her birthday. Maybe now was the time to spend it.

The next Monday morning, when Tori walked swiftly to her seat in her first class, she heard a few drawn-in breaths. It was hard not to turn around in a "snooty model" pose, with nose in the air and hand on hip, but Tori bit her lip and stared ahead at the board.

She knew exactly what she looked like, having spent all day Sunday practicing her new, slow, casual walk in front of her mirror. On Saturday afternoon the hair stylist had cut and shaped her hair into a smooth cap that made Tori's face look thinner and older. She had shown her how to use just a touch of eyebrow pencil to give her brows a neater line, and a touch of shadow to make her eyes look wider.

Tori had talked to her about using shadow and rouge to touch up her cheekbones, but the stylist had pointed out that if she used cosmetics over all her skin, it might look too theatrical in daylight.

"I want to look — well — cool. You know, like the *Vogue* models with the sunken cheeks and long necks," Tori had said.

The stylist had studied her, then said, "You can do a lot with the way you dress, Tori. You might play around with nail polish. Try something light in a rose tone. That's very stylish. Then try on all your clothes in front of your mirror and belt in your sweaters and maybe top them with a lace collar or a ribbon. When you find a look that suits you, you'll know it."

As she had tossed her T-shirts, with their silly slogans and bright colors, into the back of her closet, she had felt no regrets. She could do without them if the "new" Victoria Baniff would appeal to Dom.

Dressed in a plain navy sweater and a navy-and-gray plaid skirt that had been not-too-welcome gifts from her grandmother, Tori knew she resembled the models in the teen fashion magazines. She had studied their pictures carefully, then rummaged through her mother's boxes of scarves and jewelry until she found exactly the same sort of accessories that they wore.

In the classroom she opened her book quietly, letting her hands, with their carefully polished nails, rest casually on her desk in clear view of everyone.

When Mr. Brown said, "No, that's not it, Carl. Victoria, can you answer that question?" Tori almost snapped, "Any lamebrain could."

Biting back the words, she stared at her manicured nails and said quietly, "Isn't it the lower house of the legislature?"

"That's right," he said. Then to her surprise, he added, "I enjoyed your performance in the play, Victoria."

The words "Some of us are born with talent" popped into her head, but she said only, "Thank you."

In the halls between classes and at lunch hour,

people kept saying, "I like your haircut, Tori," except for Cowboy, who swung his leg over the chair back, crashed into the seat, and shouted, "Did you back into a lawn mower?"

Tori started to say, "No, there are shops where they cut hair with scissors, dear. You should ask your mommy to take you to one sometime."

She heard Dom set his tray down beside her. She gave Cowboy's remark a polite laugh, then ignored him.

Dom said, "Your hair looks nice, Tori."

In her mind she saw the stylist, her hands on either side of Tori's head, turning her face this way and that, squinting at Tori from various angles the way a photographer would. Instinctively, Tori narrowed her eyes in imitation, working up the whole beauty parlor scene into a funny routine. Dom smiled as though he were waiting for her to say something. Would he think she was belittling the stylist? Tori mumbled, "Thank you," and concentrated on unwrapping her sandwich.

As there were no more stage crew jobs to do until the next play, Tori caught the bus home after school. Dom hadn't mentioned giving her a ride. She didn't know if he had his car at school. Even if he did, perhaps he was now driving Eileen home. Although he continued to sit at her table in the cafeteria at noon, he did not phone Tori on Monday or Tuesday evening. Tori found herself fighting back unexpected tears that would suddenly burn behind her eyelids. By Thursday night, when he did phone, she had made up her mind that he was no longer interested in her.

Chapter 6

He said, "I — my brother's car quit, so I haven't got wheels. You think we could go to the movies with Shirl and Cowboy this weekend?"

Had Shirl told Cowboy to ask Dom to ask Tori out, after all? Surely she wouldn't do that, when Tori specifically asked her not to. If Dom had lost interest in her, and if she couldn't win him back by herself, she couldn't go out with him.

Although she wanted to say yes, she said, "Did Cowboy suggest that?"

"No. I was going to call him but I wanted to ask you first. Why? You think they won't want us along?"

Tori let out a slow breath and her shoulders relaxed. "They won't mind."

When Dom picked Tori up on Friday night, the winter sky glittered with its clear pattern of stars. Under the street lamps the pavement gleamed with an eerie emptiness, as though it were waiting for snow. Hurrying through the cold darkness, Dom and Tori tumbled into the back seat of Cowboy's car. Dom's knee bumped against hers. His hand brushed her arm.

"Got a great Western at the Rialto," Cowboy said.

"Not a singing cowboy?" Tori groaned.

"Shucks, no, little lady, a really, truly Katherine Ross."

"Since when can she play guitar?" Tori asked.

Shirl said, "Maybe Tori and Dom would rather go to something else."

Dom said, "What do you think, Tori?"

Tori almost told him what she thought of Westerns and of people who went to them, but then she remembered that she was the "new" Tori. She said, "Sure, anything is fine."

Inside the theater Cowboy led them down the aisle to the front row. Shirl asked Dom, "Is this all right?"

Cowboy said, "Hey, this is the only place. Sit back any farther, and you're clear out of the action."

Tori thought, "Listen, birdbrain, just because you're cross-eyed and can't see six inches past your nose doesn't mean the rest of us are," but she didn't say it. Instead she quietly took her seat between Dom and Shirl, carefully arranged her coat on the seat back, removed her knit scarf, and folded it neatly in her lap. No wonder neatness and politeness went together, she thought. As long as she kept busy with slow, careful motions, her brain remained in control of her mouth.

Dom whispered, "Do you have a headache, Tori?"

"What? No. Why do you ask?"

"You're awfully quiet. I just thought maybe you didn't feel well."

A howl of protest rose in Tori but stopped behind her clenched teeth. Throughout the show, she glared at the fuzzy, too-close screen, a small smile frozen on her face as she passed the boxes of popcorn and candy back and forth between Dom and Shirl.

When they sat in the car at the drive-in after the movie, Cowboy strummed an imaginary guitar and chanted the words of the movie's theme song, a melody used to fill in the sound track during long, overland, horseback-riding scenes. "Come on, Tori," Cowboy said, "hum me an accompaniment."

Imitating the voice of the movie's lead male, Tori drawled, "Shucks, good buddy, I hardly know how to accept such a fancy in-vite."

When she snapped her fingers to keep time, the dim overhead lights of the drive-in shone through the car window and reflected off her polished nails. There, she was doing it again, she realized, behaving as though she were some silly kid who always had to have the attention.

She said, "I can't remember the tune."

"You leave your wits at home tonight, honey chile?" Cowboy asked.

How would Shirl or Eileen answer a question like that? It occurred to Tori that Cowboy never said things like that to Shirl, and she wondered why not. He always directed his jokes and insults at Tori, a point she had never before considered. Did he do that because he knew that Tori could trade him joke for joke and insult for insult? Aloud Tori said, "Maybe Dom or Shirl remembers the tune."

Shirl laughed, saying, "Not me."

Dom said, "You're the one with the good ear, Tori."

So neither of them would try. Yet Tori felt sure they both remembered the tune as well as she did. All right, she decided, if that was the way Dom thought people should act, that's what she would do.

"I guess you're on your own," she said to Cowboy. "How about passing the potato chips?"

As she drank her shake and kept her conversation polite and short, an uneasiness crept over her, an odd chill, as though her coat weren't warm enough. Her skin prickled and her chest tightened, until she felt so nervous that she couldn't think of anything at all to say to anyone.

When Cowboy let them out in front of Tori's house, Dom and Tori walked slowly up the walk. He caught her hand and twined his fingers through hers. "I'll phone tomorrow," he said. "Maybe my brother's car will be fixed."

"All right," Tori said.

"Will you be home?"

"I'm not sure. I mean, maybe I'll go shopping with Mom, but I'll be home sometime."

"Umm-hmm. Tori?"

She stopped on the walk and looked up at him. Although his face was a shadow in the darkness, she could see his light hair silhouetted against the star-dotted sky. Trying to imagine Eileen's cool, slow smile, Tori kept her mouth closed and, she hoped, softly curved in a sophisticated expression.

Dom said, "Are you mad about something?"

She felt her eyes widen. She had not expected a lot of silly love talk, like the junk on the TV sitcoms, but she had at least expected something slightly romantic.

"Mad?" she blurted. "Why should I be?"

"I don't know. It's just — you've been so quiet tonight. I thought maybe — oh, never mind."

At first Tori tried to make a joke of it, saying lightly, "No, I don't have a headache, and I don't remember the tune, and I'm not mad at anyone."

"What are you talking about?"

"Well, it's just — well, Dom, you kept asking — all evening — " Tori's voice deepened in an imitation of Dom, saying, "Do you have a headache, Tori? Do you feel well, Tori? Should we order fries? Tell me what to order, when to phone, tell me how that tune went, tell me if you're mad, entertain me, Tori, but be a perfect lady like gorgeous Eileen!"

She heard her own voice rush on, uncontrolled, and stopped in shocked silence.

Dom said quietly, "Is that what you think?"

There was nothing, nothing in the whole world that she could say to take back the stupid words that had spilled out. Even if he forgave her for imitating him, he would not forget what she had said. She had made Dom sound stupid and boring when, in truth, he was only trying to be kind. And she had made that remark about Eileen. He would think that she was jealous of the attention he showed Eileen.

Tori ran up the stairs, pulled open her front door, and slammed into the house, leaving Dom outside on the walk.

Her parents were sitting in the front room, watching TV. Her mother said, "Hi, have a nice time?"

Tori forced herself to say cheerfully, "Yes, great!"

"You should have invited Dom in."

"Oh! He — Cowboy's giving him a ride. They were in a hurry."

Her mother turned back to the TV. Tori ran into her room, closed the door quietly, and then sank down on her bed and stared unseeingly at the posters on her wall. The hot tears overflowed at the corners of her eyes.

Chapter 7

In American history class on Monday morning, Tori sat at her desk smiling politely at Mr. Brown, who was explaining the civics lessons for the week. The winter sun's rays, slanted beneath the half-lowered window shades were obscuring Mr. Brown's neatly chalked outline.

Surrounding the rim of the chalkboard was a bulletin board with charts of government organizations and posters of the state capitol buildings and of Washington, D.C. While she studied each poster as though she had not seen it every day for the past eight weeks, Tori let one hand drop carefully to her side, her palm turned toward the seat behind her. She felt fingers touch her hand and then the note that she had held was gone. She returned her hand slowly to her lap, smoothing her navy skirt over her knees.

There was nothing more she could do. Now it was up to Dom. She had done what she and Shirl had decided was the only thing she could do. She had written on a small piece of paper the words, "I'm sorry," folded it over and written Dom's name on the outside, and sent it to him at the first opportunity.

"Maybe you could phone him," Shirl had suggested, but Tori had said that she could not. She could not even hand him the note herself.

There was no way that he could ever feel the same about her, think of her as a girlfriend, if he ever had. But at least she didn't want him to think that he deserved to be imitated or put down. Shirl had said, "It'll work out, Tori. He won't stay mad at you. Dom isn't the type to hold grudges."

No, he wasn't, Tori knew. He would go right on being friendly, eating lunch with them, probably helping with the next play, and occasionally phoning her about a math problem. But he would never, ever think now that Tori could be the kind of girl she knew he admired — a polite, quiet, ladylike girl. From her outburst he knew that behind the neat new hairstyle and clothes, she was still the same old show-off Tori, a girl he could like as a friend but not as a girlfriend.

Still, in the back of her mind, where she tried to ignore it, lingered some small hope that he could overlook her insults to himself and to Eileen.

He did not send any note in answer.

At noon he ate elsewhere. Tori glanced around the lunch room, trying to look casual and unconcerned, while her eyes studied every table. She didn't see him anywhere.

Shirl whispered, "Don't worry. He'll probably phone you tonight."

"No, he won't. If he won't eat lunch with me, he won't phone later," Tori mumbled, afraid her voice would break.

Chapter 7

Shirl's lower lip quivered.

Tori giggled, then sniffed and blinked her eyes rapidly to push back the tears. "It's me who should cry, not you."

"I can't stand to see you unhappy."

"I'm okay," Tori lied.

After lunch hour, as she hurried down the hall to her next class, Tori saw Dom standing at the far end of the corridor by the glass door that led to the practice field. He was listening to a group of students who stood around him. At his side, her back to the corridor, stood Eileen, her head turned as though she were looking at Dom, her dark hair shining in neat waves.

Tori ducked her head and hurried past, hoping he would not notice her. She knew that she could not say, "Hi, Dom," in the same casual way that she could shout "Hi" to any of the others, at least not today. She had made her apology in writing. Now she wished she hadn't.

What if he came up to her and said, "I got your note," and then waited for her to explain it? What more could she say, without letting it show all over her face how much she cared for him, how much she wanted him to forgive her, how much she wished the last two weeks hadn't happened, and that she could turn time back to before the play. If only it could be like that again, with the two of them alone in the storeroom cleaning up props and joking and getting to know each other.

Her afternoon classes blurred by until the last bell rang. He had made it very clear when he didn't join their table for lunch that he not only couldn't forgive her, he didn't even want to talk to her or be casual friends. Over and over she heard herself imitating him on the front walk, while the cold and the stars pressed in around them. She shivered violently and was startled to find herself sitting alone in her last class of the day, the rest of the class already rushing down the aisles and out the door, to beat the locker area jam and make it to the buses on time.

Slowly Tori slid out of her seat, gathered her books, and started down the hall. People shouted their good-byes to her. She nodded automatically, not seeing who they were, until beyond the crowd she saw the top of Dom's head. He was walking toward her. What would she say when he came even with her, saw her, and could hardly avoid speaking to her? The thought brought a tight, hard lump to her throat, blocking her voice. In panic, she darted through the nearby doorway to the auditorium, hurried past the empty seats, and ducked into the storeroom, carefully closing the door behind herself.

Her eyes burned. Tori dropped her books on the floor and let the angry tears trace their paths down her face. She knew of no way to stop them. Here in the storeroom it didn't matter.

When they finally slowed, she dug into her purse for a tissue, blew her nose, then put her hands on the sink counter and hoisted herself up, until she was sitting on the ledge with her feet in the dry sink. She leaned back against the wall of shelves and stared out the window, past its dusty metal safety screen.

Chapter 7

The road behind the school was empty. The buses had all pulled out. The only people left in school would be the team members practicing in the gym or small groups of students working on after-school committees in the scattered classrooms. Later, when she felt better, she would wander down the hall and see if there was anyone around who was driving home in her direction. If not, she could walk to the library, phone her mom at her office, and ask her to stop by the library on her way home from work.

The doorknob rattled. Tori froze, staring at it. The door opened slowly. Dom poked his head around the edge, saw her, stepped in, and closed the door behind him. As Tori turned her back to him to stare out the window, she brushed angrily at her cheeks with the palms of her hands. She knew her eyes must be red.

She heard him moving behind her, walking a few steps, leaning against the shelves. Even after he stopped moving and waited silently, she could feel him standing behind her. It seemed to Tori that the silence went on for hours.

Finally she said, "What are you doing here?"

"Looking for you," he said.

"So you've found me," she snapped. "Now you can go away."

He said softly, "Hey, Tori, don't act like that."

Tori swung around to face him, her hands gripping the counter ledge, her legs dangling. She felt the blood rising to her flaming cheeks. She burst out, "Don't tell me how to act. I know how I should act, only I can't! I tried and I can't!"

He stammered, "I didn't mean — I only meant — hey, can we talk a little, Tori?"

"There's nothing to talk about. I don't want to talk. Not to you, not to anyone. I came in here to be alone."

He glanced at the door as though he might leave, then frowned and glared back at her. "Okay, don't talk to me. Just listen for half a second and then I'll go. I got your note and, well, you don't need to apologize to me."

Tori bit her lip and said nothing, afraid she would say the wrong thing. She had written him the note because she knew she could not speak her apology. Somehow, no matter what she started out to say, the words changed by themselves, and she ended up saying the wrong thing. She couldn't trust herself to speak to Dom. She had used up the last bit of her courage when she wrote the note and then waited for him at the lunch table at noon.

Dom said, "I've been thinking a lot about, well, everything. Friday night you were trying to be someone different. Someone else."

Tori sniffed and stared at the floor. "I wasn't trying to be someone else. I was trying to be the new me."

"What's wrong with the old you?" he asked, and he sounded honestly surprised, as though he didn't know.

"Everything! I'm mean and sarcastic and always showing off."

"You say funny things and make people laugh."

"Yeah, and then I say dumb things and hurt their feelings."

"That's more than I can do. I can't walk into a room full of strangers without feeling scared."

"Scared?" Tori looked up at him and blurted, "You're almost six feet tall!"

He smiled. "Not that kind of scared. Just — embarrassed because I don't know how to — how to start talking to anybody until I've known them a long time. I never would have gone out for the stage crew if you hadn't asked me."

"I don't have any trouble talking. I just can't shut up."

"Don't put yourself down," he said.

"It's true! I can't help it. It's the way I am! And the more different I try to be, the more I'm the same. I tried, I really tried! I tried to act like Shirl, always thinking before opening my big mouth, always saying what's polite instead of what pops into my head. I wanted to be the kind of girl you'd like, only I can't do that. I can't be somebody else." Embarrassed by the words that tumbled out, Tori jumped down from the counter and stage crew if you hadn't asked me."

He reached out, caught her, and pulled her around to face him. "I don't want you to be somebody else."

Tori felt as though she would explode inside, torn between wanting to put her arms around him and thinking she really should pull free and run away. She banged her forehead against his chest, crying, "You do! You do! You want me to be like Eileen!"

To her surprise, he laughed. He tightened his arms around her, the way he had done when they were dancing at the party, bent his neck, and pressed his face against hers. He whispered, "Hey, Tori, you're crazy. Why should I want you to be like Eileen?"

Tori muttered into his sweater, "You were mad when I made fun of her at the party. I didn't mean to insult her, it just happened."

"I know that now."

"Yeah, but it'll happen again. I'm trying not to insult people, but the words pop out. I can't be like Shirl."

"I don't want you to be like Shirl. Or Eileen. Or anybody else. I want you to be Tori."

"Which Tori?" Tori demanded. "The new one? Let me tell you, I am sick of these stupid clothes. I can't sit on the floor in this dumb skirt because it has to be dry cleaned. And this junk on my eyes! It makes my lashes stick together. And do you know what a pain it is to use hair spray every morning?"

He moved his face against her hair. "Is that what smells sweet?"

"Breathe deep and you'll pass out."

Dom said, "It's gonna be harder for me. I might get away with dyeing my hair red, but I don't think I can ever learn to sing."

Tori pulled back from him, not enough to make him drop his arms, but enough to allow her to stare up into his face. "What are you talking about?"

"How do you think I feel around Cowboy? He knows how to do everything. If you're going to be like Shirl, I'll have to be like Cowboy."

"But I don't want you to be like Cowboy!" Tori wailed. "Oh, I wish we could go back and erase the last couple of weeks."

"And start all over?"

In a small voice, Tori said, "Could we?"

"Clear back at the beginning?" He sounded unsure.

"Why not?"

"I gotta work up the nerve to ask you out all over again?" He kept his voice even, but Tori knew he was fighting back a smile.

Tori giggled. "Not that far back."

"Two days later?"

"What happened two days later?"

"I dunno. I just thought we might start there."

"You're crazier than I am!"

As Dom wrapped his arms around her shoulders, Tori slid her arms around his waist. He pressed his face against hers and said, "Yeah, well, love makes people kind of crazy, I guess."

Chapter 1

Sandy blew on the callus on her left palm, then slapped her hand back on the oar. Shoving her bare feet against the damp sides of her dinghy for leverage, she leaned easily into her stroke. The oars slipped beneath the water, rose, and dripped diamond sprays from their tips.

Turning her head to look over her shoulder to check her course, Sandy spotted Pirate Rock, a mound of trees in the middle of Sunset Bay, directly in her line. She glanced back at her home shoreline, hoping to see Greg.

Madronas hung out over the water's edge, their trunks peeling from cinnamon brown to pale green, their dark leaves shimmering in the sun. She could see the rows of floating docks and, above them, the patches of lawn and house roofs between the trees. She could even see Greg Johnson's dock, half a mile down the beach from hers. Sandy squinted into the reflected light of the water.

Nothing moved on the Johnson dock. Greg's boat was tied in place. So — Greg had missed another day's practice.

"It doesn't matter," she said aloud to herself. "Greg's probably in better shape than I am. He can make it without so much training."

Channeling her anger into her stroke, Sandy clamped her hands around the oars until her knuckles stuck out in rigid mounds and strained against the steady resistance of the water, concentrating all her thoughts and effort on her rowing. By the time she had rounded Pirate Rock three times, she felt calm enough to head home at an easier pace.

Her arms and legs, stretched out in front of her in the dinghy, were long, firm, and tanned. Her black hair framed her thin face. The summer sun had traced a shiny red line across her wide cheekbones and uptilted nose, underlining her hazel eyes.

As she neared her dock, she heard her friend Jim shout, "Hi, Sandy!"

"Hi, Jimmy!" she shouted back, watching the dock over her shoulder.

Jim waved and hurried down the ramp, a solid, sun-browned shape in T-shirt and cutoffs. Squatting on the dock, he leaned out and grabbed the bow, pulling the dinghy alongside. While Jim tied up the line, Sandy lifted the oars from the oarlocks, swung them onto the dock and scrambled after them. Shouldering the oars, she carried them up the ramp to the lawn to lean them against a tree. Then she clasped her hands above her head, stretched first upward, then to each side, loosening the knots in her back and shoulders.

"You're really moving out there," Jim said. "I think you're picking up speed."

"Am I? I did my full two hours and I don't feel tired. I think I'll be in good shape for the race."

Every August the community's boating enthusiasts sponsored a race from Alki Point in Seattle to the Winslow dock, a distance of about seven miles across Puget Sound. The race was open to all comers with one limitation. Each craft had to be human-powered and could have neither sail nor motor. The crafts could be any size or type and were divided into men's and women's singles, mixed crews, and miscellaneous. This last category was reserved for the occasional raft or bicycle-powered boat that invariably appeared for laughs. Every entrant received a souvenir T-shirt, but otherwise, there were no prizes. Hundreds of people entered for the same reason that attracted Sandy. It was a challenge. What she wanted, more than trophies or glory, was to prove to herself that she could row the seven miles across the unpredictable waters of the open sound. The calm bay, protected from the winds that sometimes raised whitecaps on the sound, could not offer the same challenge.

"I've been watching you for the last half hour," Jim said.

"Too bad you can't come along."

Jim tossed his head to swing his straight blond hair out of his eyes. "I get seasick sitting on the dock."

"I know. But it gets kind of boring by myself."

"Didn't Greg show today?"

"No." If only Greg were as dependable as Jim, Sandy thought. Although Greg planned to enter the race, too, he had practiced only twice in the last week. Jim, on the other hand, showed up every day to see how she was doing, even though he couldn't tolerate the motion of a boat.

"I thought maybe he'd been out earlier," Jim said.

"Come on." Sandy tried not to let her disappointment with Greg show in her voice. "I'm thirsty. Let's go get some cider."

She led the way to the house, opened the screen door, and pattered barefoot across the kitchen linoleum to the refrigerator. Jim lifted glasses down from the cupboard. They had been neighbors for so many years that they were "at home" in each other's houses.

After carrying the cider bottle and glasses to the porch, Sandy and Jim sat on the wood steps in the shade. The overhead sun blazed through the trees, casting bright patterns across the lawn. Sandy filled their glasses, put the jug down, and rubbed her damp hands on her cutoffs. "You going to the party tonight?"

Jim shrugged. "Don't think so. Don't think I'll have a car."

"You can ride with Greg and me."

"Oh — well, no thanks, I have a bunch of stuff to do."

"Like what?" Sandy insisted. Her mother sometimes scolded her, saying Sandy henpecked Jim as though he were her kid brother instead of a neighbor her own age. But Sandy knew that Jim didn't mind. They'd been friends for so long. For years they had even checked their height together on Sandy's kitchen door-frame, measuring each other with a ruler balanced on the top of the head. Sometimes they stood on each other's feet to prevent cheating. Sandy had penciled their initials next to their height marks on the wood. She had always been taller than him, right through grade school and junior high. When had they stopped marking their height? she wondered.

Jim looked past her to the water, his blue eyes serious in his square face. He said, "I promised Mom I'd start painting the window trim today."

"You're not going to paint all night!"

"I — listen, if I get done I'll be at the party, but anyhow, my uncle might be dropping by this evening so it all depends."

"Do you want Greg and me to pick you up or not?" she demanded.

"No, I don't. If I can make it, I'll get there." Jim stood up. "I guess I better get started. Thanks for the cider." He bolted down the steps.

Sandy watched him hurry across the lawn and down the ramp, smiling to herself at his gait. He moved lightly on his feet, almost bouncing. Going down the slope of the ramp, he turned his knees out. Now she remembered when they'd stopped measuring their heights together. It had been three years ago, the summer of their freshman year in high school, when her mark was two inches higher than Jim's. Now when they faced each other, their eyes were even, so she guessed he had finally caught up with her.

Returning to the kitchen, Sandy put away the clean dishes from the dishwasher. Then she pulled the vacuum from the closet and ran it through the downstairs rooms. With her chores finished, she dashed upstairs to take her shower.

As she came out of the bathroom, one towel wrapped around her head, the other around her body, she heard the front door slam.

"Sandy, have you had lunch yet?" her mother called.

"No."

Her mother walked out of the kitchen and stood at the bottom of the stairs, looking up at her. "I left the groceries on the counter. Put them away, will you, dear? Izzy and Andrea are over at MacPherson's for lunch and I've got to run. I'm late."

"Okay, Mom. See ya." Sandy was relieved that her younger sisters wouldn't be home for lunch. If they were staying at MacPherson's they'd stay most of the afternoon. They wouldn't be sitting around on the porch whining, "What can we *do*, Sandy? There's nothing to do!" And they wouldn't be leaving trails of comic books and discarded shoes and towels all over the house for her to pick up.

As much as Sandy loved summer vacation, it did have one drawback. With both of her parents working all day, Sandy, being the oldest, was responsible for her two younger sisters and the condition in which they left the house.

Sitting down at her dressing table, Sandy rubbed her hair half-dry with her towel, then combed it straight. She scowled at her jagged fingernails. Whatever rowing might be doing to keep her body in shape, it was certainly ruining her hands. Should she bother to work on them?

Why not, she decided. With her sisters gone, she had a little time to do something extra for herself. After filing her nails smooth with an emery board, she pushed back the cuticles with the side of her nail file. She had to keep her nails short for rowing, but at least they didn't have to look as though she used them to scrape barnacles off her boat. Sandy smoothed hand lotion from her wrists to fingertips, rubbing it into her hardened palms, smiling at the thick layer of calluses. They were clear proof of her long hours of rowing practice.

This summer would be the best ever, Sandy thought. First, this was the first year her parents had agreed that she was old enough to enter the cross-sound race. Second, Greg planned to enter, too. And third, there was Greg himself. Although Sandy had known Greg's family since they moved to Sunset Bay two years ago, she hadn't paid much attention to Greg until this spring when he began to pay attention to her. Then she wondered how she could have missed noticing how special he was.

A slight frown drew her dark eyebrows together. When she and Greg had first agreed to enter the race, they'd practiced rowing after school every day in every kind of April weather except downpour. By May, Greg had begun to skip as often as he showed up. Of course, he was a senior, a year ahead of Sandy, with final exams and graduation activities, and Sandy had understood that. She had hoped he hadn't changed his mind about the race.

Certainly he hadn't changed about anything else. He took her to all the parties.

Chapter 1

When Greg arrived that evening, Sandy and Isabel were clearing away the supper dishes. Sandy heard the car turn into the drive. The door slammed and Greg's heavy footsteps thumped up the steps to the house.

Nine-year-old Andrea shouted, "Sandy, your lover boy is here!"

Izzy, who would start junior high school that September, hissed, "Shut up, Andrea! He'll hear you!"

Sandy smiled. A year ago Izzy would have joined Andrea's shouting. This year Izzy had suddenly become shy whenever a boy came near her, looking at her feet and speaking very softly and carefully. To Sandy's complete surprise and bafflement, Isabel even acted that way around Jim.

She could better understand Izzy's awe of Greg. He really was something. She tucked her T-shirt into her jeans and ran to open the door. "Hi, Greg, I'll be right out."

From the front room her mother called, "Hello, Greg."

He stuck his head in the door and said, "Hi, Mrs. Stevens."

Sandy's father called, "Got any bets on the Mariners?"

Greg said, "They'll win easy."

Sandy said, "Don't you start on baseball with Dad or we'll never get away," and pushed him out the door. Greg had played varsity basketball and could talk sports for hours.

"Don't be too late," her father called.

"I won't," she shouted back.

Greg waited for her by the car. "Should we pick up Jim?"

"No, he said not to stop for him."

Greg smiled. "You mean I get you all to myself tonight?"

Sandy's heart did that nervous thing it always did when Greg smiled that way. She didn't know whether to blame her heart or his smile, but probably it was his fault because nobody else's smile gave her any trouble. As Andrea was fond of pointing out, Greg was "cute-cute-cute!" He was tall and athletic, with wavy black hair, dark brown eyes, and strong, well-shaped features.

Sandy said quickly, "Where were you this morning?"

"Third degree time?" he teased. "Sorry, I really meant to row this morning, only I overslept."

"That's an excuse?" She slid into the car beside him.

He laughed and brushed his fingertips along the side of her face, saying, "I'll be there tomorrow for sure, unless you keep me out too late tonight."

Chapter 2

The party, held at Chandler's beach, almost blocked the access road with its overflow of cars. Everything from old jalopies to the latest model cars were parked at angles to fit the uneven gravel shoulder. Wedged between tree clumps, their front bumpers pressed into tangled growths of dark ferns. Leaving the car half off the road at the first empty spot, Greg and Sandy headed down the beach path, their arms loaded with grocery sacks.

"Why do we bring this junk?" Sandy asked, peering into her sack. "We never eat it."

Greg said, "Speak for yourself, I'm starved."

"Didn't you have supper?"

"Unh-uh. Mom's over at Gran's."

The path wound between the straight, dark trunks of the towering firs — a cleared dirt trail half-lost in the lush green shadows of the thick branches far overhead. Wild salal shrubs tumbled over the path's edge. Their sticky, purple black berries were hanging like miniature lanterns from arched stems, reaching out for the few stray wisps of late sun rays that penetrated the woods. Where the trees stopped abruptly at the line drawn by saltwater seepage, the trail ended in a narrow meadow of beach grass which in turn ended at the high tide line, a line marked by rows of silvery driftwood. Beyond the old logs stretched a pattern of coarse gravel and sand, pale and dry in the evening sunset except at its lower edge where the salt water stirred restlessly.

Piles of twigs and dry branches, scavenged from between the logs, crackled with the beginnings of a fire, while a circle stood around waiting to add larger pieces of wood. The heavy-sweet aroma of wood smoke mingled with the sharp smell of the sea and the pungent fragrance of the forest. Sandy took a deep breath and sighed, "I could make a meal of that smell."

Greg said, "Terrific. That's three more hot dogs for me."

Friends waved to them, shouting, "Bring on the goodies! Whatcha got?"

Greg said, "Would you believe three pounds of store-bought cookies; two jars of pickles; one bottle each of catsup, mustard, and a barbecue sauce for fire-eaters; six sacks of chips; and enough pop to rot five hundred teeth?"

"Of you I'd believe anything," Mary Jo said. "From Sandy I expected something better."

Sandy set the grocery bags down on a log. "Like what?"

"Maybe something home-baked?"

Frank said, "Can't build rowing muscle in the kitchen, huh, Sandy?"

"How's it going? You both still planning on the race?" someone else asked.

Chapter 2

"Planning on it! We're gonna win it!" Greg said. "Sandy will win the women's singles and I'll win the men's."

"Keeping it in the family?" Mary Jo asked.

Greg draped his arm around Sandy's shoulders, pulling her against him. "You better believe it!"

"Still rowing every day?"

Sandy said, "I'm up to two hours. Haven't missed a day since school closed."

"You're something else," Frank said. "All I've done this summer is sleep."

His girlfriend, Marta, reached out to pat his stomach and said, "And eat."

Frank squealed in a mock falsetto, "Keep your hands off me, you fresh thing!"

Greg dug two marshmallows out of a bag, pressed them onto a toasting fork and held them to the fire. Sandy watched the white edges crinkle slowly in a ring of bubbles, fade to a golden brown, and then melt into a rounder shape. Greg held out the fork to her. Pinching lightly at the marshmallows to loosen them from the fork, Sandy waited a moment for them to cool, grasped one, and slid it off the fork prongs. While Greg removed the other one, Sandy popped hers in her mouth, biting through the crisp outer layer to the sticky center.

"You're a fabulous cook," she mumbled around a mouthful.

"That's only half my repertoire. I also know how to burn hot dogs. Want a demonstration?"

"Wouldn't miss it!"

"Okay, you asked for it. Watch this." Greg

pressed a wiener onto the fork, flourished it above his head like a sword, and then held it out over the flames.

"It may not taste like much, but I admire your style," Sandy said.

Frank said, "Greg, you got a job yet?"

"Just Wednesdays at the warehouse. How about you?"

"Dishwashing two nights a week at the coffee shop. But I don't care, it's only for the summer. I'm going to community college next fall."

"In Seattle?"

"Yeah. Listen, if four or five of us go, we could maybe split costs on a car. You interested?"

Greg shrugged and squatted down by the fire, carefully turning the wieners above the flame. "I dunno. I can't think about school. We just got out. I'm not crazy about going back."

"Beats washing dishes."

"Anything beats washing dishes," Sandy agreed. "Have you picked a major, Frank?"

"I thought I'd try computer programming. I'm pretty good at math. If I make it through, the money's good, they say. Of course, if Marta'd keep working I could marry her for her money and forget the whole thing."

"Fat chance," Marta said.

Sandy knew that Marta had been cashiering at the drugstore since graduation. She asked, "Are you going to quit your job?"

"I'm just working this summer to save enough to go to college in September."

"You going into computers, too?"

"Can't decide. I guess I'll just start and then see what I like."

Frank said, "There, Sandy, see how lucky you are? A whole year more of high school and security and Mom's apple pie before you're cast into the cold world to make your own decisions."

"Here you are," Greg said, holding out the cooked wiener on the fork.

After Sandy slid the wiener onto the bun, she stopped with her knife in the pickle relish jar, stood motionless, and watched the sun drop behind the jagged blue line of the Olympic Mountains. This beach, like her own, faced west toward the Kitsap Peninsula, the Olympic Peninsula. Past the mountains and over the horizon curve was the Pacific Ocean. For a few seconds the sun seemed to hesitate, a bright red dot of flame resting in a crevice of the mountain peaks, then disappeared. It left the sky above it pale blue, coloring the undersides of a lone cloud a brilliant golden pink.

Sandy glanced at her watch — almost ten o'clock. She wondered what it would be like to live in northern Alaska where the sun stayed above the horizon all night during midsummer.

Beside her, Greg said, "There's Jim."

Still dressed in his cutoffs and T-shirt, Jim stood out against the dark trees at the path's end. Sandy waved and yelled.

Jim walked slowly toward them carrying a box.

"What've you got?" Mary Jo shouted.

Jim didn't answer until he reached the logs. Then he grinned and said, "Chocolate cake."

Everyone applauded.

"Good old dependable Jim," Marta said.

Jim handed Marta the cake, then climbed among the logs scavenging wood to add to the fire. As the sky darkened, small groups that had wandered down the beach to wade in the shallow water now drifted back to the fire. There were more than twenty people at the party. They took turns eating and singing and telling jokes. Sandy sat on a log next to Greg, her arm around his waist, his arm around her shoulders, swaying in time to the music. After pushing more logs into the fire, Jim stared into the flames, his face reflecting the glow so that Sandy could see his frown.

"What's the matter, Jimmy?" she called.

He looked up, surprised, then grinned. "Nothing."

"You look so solemn."

"Yeah, well, I gotta be leaving in an hour or so."

"The party's just starting," Greg said. "What else have you got to do?"

"I'm painting the house, and when I get ours done I've got a couple of other offers."

"To paint houses?"

"Yeah."

"Pay much?"

"I hope so," Jim said.

Greg pulled Sandy to her feet, saying, "Come on, babe, let's go wading."

"That water's ice!"

"You've got all that cake inside you to keep you warm."

Chapter 2

"Hey, that's right. The cake was great, Jim," Sandy called back over her shoulder as Greg dragged her toward the water.

Jim smiled but didn't answer, his face again turned to the flames.

Greg and Sandy kicked off their shoes and wandered at the water's edge, ducking in and out of the icy swirls, letting it cover their feet. Where the incoming waves broke on the shore, they shimmered like starlight, the phosphorescence in the water turning the foam to silver. Sandy darted into the foam, swung around, dashed back out, and bumped into Greg. Linking their arms around each other's waists, they ran back and forth from the dry sand to the water, splashing in and out, until they were halfway down the beach from the fire and out of sight of the others. Gasping for breath, they stopped, leaned against each other, and laughed. Greg rubbed his hands briskly up and down Sandy's arms. His fingers tightened and he pulled her closer, to kiss her mouth.

When they separated, he asked, "Still cold?"

"You're not doing a thing for my feet." She tried to sound offhand and casual, even though his kisses left her feeling special.

"Your feet are on their own, babe."

Sandy laughed, pushed free of his arms, and ran toward the water. He chased her, caught her arms, and half-carried her to its edge. "Want to go in swimming?" he teased, pushing her.

"No!" she shrieked.

"Afraid of a little water?"

"Don't you dare!"

"Dare? You daring me?"

She tried to hook her foot around his ankle, her wet skin slipping against his, while he struggled to keep his balance. He warned, "If you trip me, we both go in."

"If I get soaked, so do you!"

"Want a truce?"

"What kind of truce?"

Greg pulled her closer, hugging her against himself, and kissed her ear. Cold salt water washed over her feet. Sandy lifted her face and kissed him back. She whispered, "Okay, I've got my white flag out."

"That's better."

Holding hands they wandered back toward the fire. Their jeans were soaked up to their knees, cold and clinging to their legs. When they reached their friends, Marta called out, "Hey, there, children, no wandering off in twosies!"

"That's the best way to wander," Greg said. They stood by the crackling logs, first facing the flames, then turning their backs to the fire to try to dry out. As Sandy switched positions, she looked around the circle and chatted with whomever she faced, until she noticed that Jim wasn't there.

"Where's Jimmy?"

"He left. Said he had to get home."

As Sandy stared into the fire, wondering why Jim had left, she found her thoughts blurring, her eyelids wanting to close. She was sure she remembered him saying he had to leave in an hour, but that was only fifteen minutes ago. She shook her head and yawned. Maybe she had misunderstood him. It must be the fire making her feel so tired, she thought, until she began to notice the dull ache in her shoulders and thighs. No, it wasn't the fire, it was the rowing. Tomorrow morning she should start earlier, or else she would be out on the water when the sun was high and risk a burn. Rowing in the race would be hard enough without the pain of a sunburn.

To Greg she said, "Let's go home now."

"Now? It's early."

"Yeah, but I want to be out on the water by eight and first I've got to straighten up the kitchen and set out breakfast for my sisters."

"We just got here," Greg complained as Sandy said her good nights to everyone.

"It's almost midnight," she told Greg as she headed up the path in front of him.

"Doesn't seem like it."

"It will tomorrow when your alarm goes off."

They drove home in silence, Sandy leaning back in her seat, her eyes half-closed. She knew Greg was annoyed with her because he didn't reach over to pull her into his arm as he drove, but she was too tired to worry about it. Tomorrow, out on the water, with two hours of rowing to complete, he'd be glad he'd turned in early. At her door, she said, "Don't forget to set your alarm."

"Yes, mother." Greg looked at her as though he were studying her face, and Sandy had an odd feeling that he was wondering whether she was worth the bother.

She said, "You don't have to. I thought you wanted to practice for the race."

He said slowly, "I do want to, Sandy. Tell you what, I'm lousy with alarms. When it rings, I turn it off and fall back to sleep. How about you phone me?"

"Sure, I will."

"Keep ringing. Everybody else leaves the house by seven-thirty so I'll have to get out of bed to answer."

"I'll wait. And if you don't answer, I'll come over and pound down your door," Sandy said.

Greg kissed her, then said, "Okay, babe, go get your sleep."

Sandy knew that he was disappointed, that he had wanted to stay longer at the party, but she didn't know what else she could have done. By the time she reached her room, she could hardly stay awake long enough to change into her pajamas. As she curled around her pillow, she wished she could think of a way to make Greg understand that he didn't need to enter the race to please her, if that was his only reason. But what if she was wrong, what if he really did want to race? If she asked him, wouldn't it sound as though she didn't have confidence in his ability? Her worries mixed with her feelings about Greg, remembering his arms around her as they stood gazing at the bonfire, and Sandy's mind drifted toward sleep.

Chapter 3

Sandy woke the next morning to the fragrance of pine, sea, and sunshine that poured through her open windows. She dressed quietly, peeked in the next bedroom at her sleeping sisters and tiptoed down the stairs. While she ate her breakfast, cleaned up the kitchen, and set out cereal bowls for Izzy and Andrea, she thought about Greg.

Today would be one of those marvelous, cloudless days, clear and crisp until noon, then too warm in the sun but perfect under the trees. She wanted to finish her rowing early, but if they started at eight, they could row an hour, take a break, row another hour, and still be done by noon.

She dialed Greg's number and let it ring, mentally picturing him in bed, covering his head with a pillow, then slowly waking and stumbling downstairs to the phone.

"Hello?" His voice was heavy with sleep.

"Good morning. You awake?"

"No."

"I've got an idea. I thought maybe I could pack us a picnic, and then we could row for an hour, and then take a break on Pirate Rock? Want to?"

"Huh? Oh. Yeah, sure, fine."

"Are you sure you're awake?"

"Umm. Sure. Uh — Sandy, you go ahead. I'll be out pretty soon."

Sandy softly whistled a tune of her own invention as she packed a basket with snacks and a thermos. She carried it to the dock, did a few warm-up stretches, climbed into her dinghy, and rowed out from the dock. Her shoulders and legs felt fine, the aches gone with a night's sleep. As she leaned comfortably into her stroke, she glanced back at the house. Izzy and Andrea would sleep for another hour, wake slowly, argue with each other, and eat their cereal in front of the TV. If they needed her for anything, they knew that all they had to do was come out on the dock and shout.

Facing her dock, she rowed away from it toward the island. The water stretched around her like a mirror, broken only by the rippling wake of her oars and the boat, reflecting the pattern of trees and cottages on the bank. The sun had barely risen above the roofline of Sandy's house. It was casting long shadows down the lawn and touching the water with fingers of light that spread and widened beyond the shadows of the firs into the sparkling blue water. A flock of starlings rose together from the branches of a madrona, folded their wings to their bodies, and fell in a breathtaking arch to the beach, looking like wind-driven leaves. The only sounds to break the morning stillness were the chatter of the birds and the creaking of the oarlocks.

Chapter 3

Sandy circled Pirate Rock once and started on her second turn when she saw Greg on his dock, untying his boat. She continued her rhythmical stroke, knowing he would reach the rock at the same time she came back around it. She pulled steadily through the shadows of its north and west banks, moved into the south turn, and rowed eastward toward him. When she looked over her shoulder and saw his boat, he waved. He wore his old gray warm-ups, shrunk by numerous launderings, so that they clung to his tall form and the square, hard outline of his shoulders.

"There's a good kid," Greg said, and smiled at she trailed an oar and brought her dinghy even with his.

"Yeah, really great."

"You get any breakfast?"

"Nope."

"Well, never mind, I brought coffee."

"There's a good kid," Greg said and smiled at her, his even teeth shining in his tan face. When he looked like that, Sandy wanted to throw her arms around him and hug him.

Instead she checked her watch. "Thirty minutes to go and I'll feed you."

"Give me a number of laps. Tell you what, how about three laps, no matter what the time, and then quit."

"It won't do any good to practice speed. When we get out from shore on the sound it's going to be a steady rhythm that counts, not speed."

"Yeah, I guess so," Greg said, but he sounded unsure.

"It could rain or be choppy or anything. If it does that, you won't be able to row faster, you'll just have to buckle down."

"That sounds like that kid story about the turtle," Greg said, but he leaned into a steady stroke.

They circled the island for half an hour, then beached their boats on its west bank, tying them to a tangle of tree roots that jutted out from the dry mud above the water line.

Pirate Rock boasted a summer cabin — a three-room log structure with a fireplace of native stone — built at its highest point. The surrounding island, little more than four acres, was a jumble of silver-trunked alders and madronas and firs, with an undergrowth of huckleberry, blackberry, and ferns. Now the trees had pressed back into the clearing, seedlings had grown to lean against the cabin walls, and falling branches had destroyed most of the roof. Sandy and Greg started toward the cabin to explore, but when berry vines tore at their legs, they turned back to the south edge.

A rock jutted out into the water, catching the sunlight. Carefully avoiding the slippery patches of moss, they climbed onto its flat, sun-dried top. Sandy opened the coffee thermos while Greg unwrapped bagels filled with cream cheese and a plastic bag of washed grapes.

"I should have breakfast with you every morning," he said. "Sure beats my bowl of cereal."

"Now, aren't you glad you came out to row? You could have slept through this whole fabulous morning."

Greg laughed. "That's a hard choice."

"You mean you'd rather sleep than be out here with all this fresh air and invigorating exercise?"

"You sound like a Scout leader. I can skip the air and exercise, but I like the food."

"Okay, meet me every day and I'll provide the food."

"Not a bad deal. When we finish, you want to try for the cabin again? I feel stronger now. I'll go first and trample down the vines."

"No, we'd better do our rowing. It's going to get hot today."

"All the more reason to go explore those nice shady woods. Have you ever seen the cabin?"

Sandy said, "Sure, years ago. It's all tumbled down."

"No secret treasures hidden in the walls?"

"In log walls? Not likely. The only things hidden in the cabin are berry vines and thorns."

"Okay, then, how about staying right here in the sun? I could use a nap after breakfast."

"No, you can't," Sandy said, standing up carefully and picking her way back down the rock. At its base, she jumped off into the ferns. "Another hour to go."

"What's the hurry?" Greg slid off the rock, bumped into Sandy's back, and put his arms around her waist to catch his balance. "If you don't want to go exploring, I'm sure I can think of something else to do."

"You're thinking up excuses."

"Aw, come on," Greg said, and kissed the back of Sandy's neck.

She giggled, shrugged her shoulders, and broke loose from his hold. It would have been fun to stay in his arms, joking with him. Sandy was tempted, but she knew that if she gave in now, they would spend the rest of the day playing on the narrow gravel beach, perhaps taking a quick swim in their clothes, and then lying on the sunny rock to dry out. And tomorrow they would do the same thing, and the day after, until her determination to be in shape for the race fell apart.

She tried to keep her voice light to avoid an argument. "Some athlete you are, trying to talk me into breaking training. I've fed you, now you have to row!" She caught his hand and, laughing, pulled him toward their beached dinghies.

"Slave driver," Greg complained, as they untied their lines and pushed their boats back into the water.

"Want to go the other way around the rock?" Sandy asked.

"Sure, why not?"

Rowing slowly northward, they circled the island clockwise. An occasional bird called. From across the water they could hear sounds from cottages — the banging of screen doors, the rattle of dishes, and a child shouting a question. As the surface of the bay warmed, it smelled heavily of seaweed. After their first lap, Greg let his oars drag the water.

He called, "Sandy, I'd better head in now."

"I thought you were going to row for an hour."

"I was, but I just remembered. I'm supposed to go to town this afternoon." He rowed slowly away from her. "Thanks for the picnic. I'll see you tomorrow."

"Shall I phone you?"

"No, I'll set my alarm. I'll get up. I promise."

Sandy bit her lip to hold in her irritation. It was up to Greg, of course. He could do as he pleased. She had no right to tell him otherwise. She knew all this, thought it through sensibly, but still felt hurt that he kept making excuses. She almost wished he would come right out and say that he didn't want to be in the race. If he had so little time, he would not have wanted to explore Pirate Rock with her.

As she rowed around the island, watching the shadows change as the sun moved overhead, she fell into the spell of the water — its clean smell, the soft lapping sounds, the sparkling curve of her wake. Her senses lulled her mind until her anger died. By the time she returned to her dock, she had forgiven Greg.

Jimmy waited for her, caught the rope that she tossed to him, and held her dinghy against the dock while she climbed out. After she tied her boat and carried her oars up to the porch, Sandy said, "I've got to make lunch for Izzy and Andrea. Come on in."

"No, I'm — I left the ladder and paint out. I've gotta get back."

"How's it coming?" Sandy asked. She turned on the bottom step and looked down at Jimmy, who had stopped on the walk.

"The window frames are done. Now I'm going to start the dormer shingles."

"What happened to you last night? I thought you'd stay longer at the party."

As Jim stuck his hands into the pockets of his cutoffs and tossed his head, he avoided meeting Sandy's gaze. "I had to get the car back. Well, see you later."

"Sure you won't stay for lunch?"

"Not today. You and Greg stop out on the rock?"

"Oh, that's right! I left my thermos in the boat. We had bagels. I've got more inside, if you'd like one."

"Uh — no, thanks. I thought maybe you — uh — went to the old cabin."

"Too overgrown. We started, but the blackberries are murder."

Jim nodded, then turned and jogged across the neighbors' lawns toward his home. Sandy called, "See you, Jimmy."

When he didn't answer, she wondered if he had heard her.

Chapter 4

Although Greg phoned daily and took Sandy to the movies the following Friday, he never showed up again for morning practice. Twice Sandy thought of phoning him. She had sat by her phone with the receiver raised, chewing on a ragged fingernail. She stared out the window at the sea-gulls diving above the bay, their white V-shapes reflecting the morning sunlight. She had dialed the first three numbers. He had told her not to phone, promised that he would set his alarm, said that he would come out to practice. If she phoned, would he think that her only interest in him was in his rowing? Worse yet, he might think she pestered him about the rowing as an excuse to be near him.

Although she had looked forward to entering the cross-sound race with him, their relationship certainly did not depend on it. In fact, one thing had nothing to do with the other. She could as easily enjoy entering the race with Jimmy, who was only a friend and neighbor. She had hoped that Greg understood that she would care about him in the special way she did whether he liked to row or not.

Sandy had pressed down the phone button, cutting the connection.

When Greg showed up in his boat Monday morning, looking over his shoulder and lifting one hand from an oar to wave at her, Sandy waved back. She had been careful not to mention rowing to him on their Friday night date, after deciding that he must have wanted to drop out but was embarrassed to do so.

He stroked across the gleaming water, his oar-locks creaking, his oars trailing crystal spray, until his dinghy was beside hers. "Been out here long?"

"Almost two hours," she said. "I was about to head in."

"I guess I'm late. Well, I think I'll go ahead and row. I've got a week to make up for."

Sandy almost told him that he couldn't make up for a week in one day, then decided that he didn't need her advice. He never rowed for more than an hour, anyway, and if he practiced every day for the next week, he could still be ready for the race.

As she rowed slowly back to her dock, she watched him bend to his oars, stroking at a faster pace than she thought he could sustain for very long. Izzy and Andrea didn't give her time to worry about Greg. They were waiting at the dock, hopping up and down, chanting, "Hurry up, Sandy, you said you'd play Monopoly with us, you promised."

By the time she put away her oars and made sandwiches for their lunch, her sisters had set up a game on the grass under the canopy of trees. Andrea squatted yoga fashion, with her knees out and her ankles crossed, on her side of the game board. Izzy threw the dice, then grabbed a sandwich. Sandy joined them.

As they played, Sandy glanced constantly at the bay, watching Greg. Several times she saw him circling the east side of Pirate Rock. He had pulled off his sweat shirt and his bare back looked pale in the sunlight. She waved but he didn't look toward shore. Would he remember that they were supposed to go to town today to sign up for the race? She had planned to wait until her parents came home at five-thirty, borrow their car, and drive the five miles to town. She was sure the sign-up table in front of the grocery store would stay open until six for commuters returning from work.

The Monopoly game continued for two hours. When they quit, Greg was still rowing. Sandy helped Izzy pack up the game and put it away. Then they all sat on the dock for a while, dangling their feet in the water.

"We could dig clams," Andrea said.

"Can't either, dummy, it's too late," Izzy said.

"Is it too late, Sandy?"

Sandy hadn't seen any red tide reports in the newspaper, but they didn't usually dig clams in August, red tide infection or not. The clams tended to be too tough.

"I don't think they'd be much good now," she said. "I'll bait a hook for you, if you'd like to fish."

"I wish I had something to read," Andrea complained. "I wish we could go to the drugstore and buy some comics. I've still got my allowance."

"You wanna walk five miles, dummy?" Izzy asked.

"We could catch the bus."

"That bus only runs a couple times a day. We'd have to wait for hours!"

"Would we, Sandy?" Andrea asked.

"Would we what?" Sandy asked, her mind on Greg, worrying that he was staying out too long.

Andrea repeated her question, her eyes wide in her round face. Sometimes Sandy had the feeling that Andrea thought she had the wisdom of Solomon, and Sandy wasn't sure she wanted to live up to such a notion. Andrea stuffed the edge of her dark braid in her mouth and chewed on it, waiting for an answer.

Sandy said slowly, "I don't know the schedule. We must have something around to read. Come on, I'll help you look."

"And take your hair out of your mouth!" Izzy said.

"You mind your own business!" Andrea shouted.

"You both hush up," Sandy snapped, weary of hearing them argue.

"Oh, she thinks she's so smart!" Andrea shouted. "Just because she's going to be in junior high next year! You should see her with her friends, Sandy, all they do is poke each other and watch the boys and act silly!"

"Shut up!" Izzy screamed.

Andrea continued, "Know what she did? This morning I caught her smearing Mom's makeup all over her face!"

Izzy let out a shriek and ran into the house,

slamming the door behind her. Sandy gave Andrea's braid a soft tug. She said, "Hey, that's not nice, always fighting."

"Well, she did!"

"So what? It's none of your business. When you're that old, maybe you'll want to try makeup, too."

"Never!" Andrea exclaimed. "It's so dumb."

"Never mind. Come on. I've got a Tarzan book around somewhere."

After she found the Tarzan book and sent Andrea outside to read under the tree, Sandy knocked lightly on Izzy's bedroom door. She called softly, "It's me. Can I come in?"

She heard Izzy sniff and mumble something, so she opened the door. Izzy stood by the window, staring out at the trees, her hands pressed against her face.

"Hey, what's the matter?" Sandy asked. "Since when do you let Andrea get you down?"

Izzy faced her, wailing, "It's not Andrea, it's me! Look at me! I'm a mess! I'm ugly and skinny and nobody likes me!"

Sandy stared with dismay at her young sister. Izzy's pale, thin face reminded her of herself at that age, with circles beneath her eyes and her upper teeth protruding slightly. Her hair hung in limp tendrils that only hinted at the natural curl.

"You're not ugly!" Sandy exclaimed. "Hey, you know, my teeth were just like that before I got my braces! I'd forgotten. After the dentist puts bands on them, you'll be surprised how fast they straighten."

"I don't want to go to school with braces!"

Sandy tried not to laugh. "As I remember it, when I was in junior high, people who didn't have braces were real weirdos! Everybody had them."

Izzy's mouth trembled between crying and laughing. "Yeah, I suppose so, but why me?"

"That's what we all ask. Listen, honey, the only thing wrong with you is that your hair is getting more oily so you really ought to wash it every day, like I do. Come on, I'll give you a shampoo and blow-dry, if you want, and you'll see, it'll look nice."

"It won't ever be curly like yours! I'll never be as pretty as you or have a boyfriend like Greg."

"Don't you believe that," Sandy said as she steered Izzy toward the sink. "Your hair is wavy, and you can fix it a lot of ways."

A half hour later, after she had finished Izzy's hair and found her a paperback to read, she wandered down to the dock to see if Greg's boat was tied up. If he were home, she thought, she ought to phone him to remind him about the sign-up.

To her surprise, his boat was not at his dock. Sandy held her hand above her eyes and squinted into the glare from the water. Greg still circled the island, rowing more slowly now, but keeping up a steady rhythm. Sandy waved both arms above her head and shouted his name. He didn't hear her.

She felt the dock shake beneath her feet as Jim jogged down the ramp to stand beside her. "Been out there awful long, hasn't he?"

"Three and a half hours," Sandy said.

"What for? Even in a storm, it can't take more than two hours to cross the sound. If it's worse weather than that, they'll cancel the race."

"I guess he wants to be sure he's in shape," Sandy said weakly, not really knowing why Greg was staying out so long.

"I thought maybe he'd changed his mind about racing."

"Me, too, but I guess not, Jimmy."

"Don't you have to sign up today?"

"Yes. Well, I'm not sure Greg knows."

"I think he's coming in now."

They watched Greg swing his boat shoreward, still rowing steadily. Sandy said, "I'll go over to remind him about the sign-up. Want to come along?"

"Unh-uh. Gotta get back to work."

With the water at low tide, the mud bank beneath the lawns lay drying in the sun, smelling of shellfish and seaweed. It made funny popping sounds beneath Sandy's feet as she ran in front of the neighbors' lawns until she reached Greg's place. She walked out on his dock in time to catch the line he tossed. After winding it around the post, she knelt on the dock to hold his dinghy still.

"Do I get this service every day?" Greg's smile looked forced, as though he were very tired.

"I came over to remind you that we have to sign up this afternoon."

"Now?" As he climbed out of his boat, carrying his oars, he swayed unsteadily. Sandy caught his arm.

"You okay?"

"Beat," he admitted. "I gotta go stand in a hot shower."

"I was going to town around five-thirty."

"Yeah, well, listen, could you sign up for me, too?"

"I think so."

"Okay, do that. Thanks, babe." Greg staggered up the lawn toward his house. His shoulders glowed with uneven red streaks.

"You look like you've got a sunburn," Sandy called. "Better put something on it."

Greg nodded but didn't answer. Sandy turned slowly and wandered down the shore until she reached her own lawn. Izzy and Andrea were still stretched out under the trees with their books. Sandy walked up to the house, turned on the garden hose, and washed off her feet. Chilling her ankles, the cold water traced rivulets of mud across her feet. As she sat on the steps and tied on her tennis sneakers, she gazed up at the fir branches with their heavy clusters of greenish brown cones. She thought about finding a book for herself, decided she was too restless to read, and wandered across the adjoining lawn to Jim's house. She spotted him on the ladder, painting the shingles on the upstairs dormer.

"Can I help?" she called.

He looked down, surprised. "Aren't you going to town?"

"Greg's too tired, so I'll have to wait till my folks get home."

Jim nodded, then backed down the ladder carrying his paint can and brush. When he reached the ground, he said, "I can drive you in, if you want."

"You're busy with painting."

"No, I'm at a good stopping place. Put this stuff in the shed for me, and I'll go get the keys."

"I can't leave Izzy and Andrea alone."

"They can go, too." Jim ran lightly up the steps and disappeared through the screen door.

Sandy carried the paint can and brush to the shed, stepped on the can lid to press it closed, then left the brush in an open coffee can filled with turpentine. When Jim shouted at her, she hurried out to the driveway and climbed into his father's old truck.

"I didn't come over to beg a ride," she said.

Jim grinned. "Sure you did."

"I did not!"

"Yeah, that's your story."

"Jim!" Sandy slapped his arm.

"Look out, don't hit the driver!"

"You just wanted an excuse to quit painting."

Jim laughed, his blue eyes crinkling at the edges, and Sandy noticed the tiny dots of white paint, scattered like freckles across his square face.

"You painting yourself or the house?" she demanded. He glanced down at his arms. Sandy followed his glance and saw the paint spatters on his T-shirt and cutoffs, as well as on his sun-tanned arms, legs, and feet.

"How can you drive without shoes?"

Jim turned the truck into her yard. "We all got different talents," he said, leaning on the horn.

Sandy's sisters, buried in their books, either

didn't hear the horn or chose to ignore it, not thinking it might be for them. After waiting a minute, Sandy went around the house to fetch them from under the tree. They followed her back to the truck, delighted to have a ride to town.

"Could you drop us off at the drugstore while you go to the sign-up?" they asked Jim.

When he said he would, they climbed in the cab, Andrea sitting on Izzy's lap, pushing Sandy into the center where she was pressed against Jim.

"Move your knee or I can't shift gears," he said.

"I'll keep my knee out of your gears if you keep your elbow out of my ribs," Sandy said.

"It's a deal," Jim said.

Andrea said, "Better not get too close or Greg'll be jealous!"

"Don't talk dumb!" Izzy hissed.

"Well, he will," Andrea insisted. "He will so, 'cause Jim's a boy."

Jim said, "Gee, I'm glad you noticed."

Andrea giggled and Izzy blushed furiously. They drove east on the highway to Winslow, a small town on the western shore of Puget Sound, about seven miles across the water from Seattle. The race would start on the Seattle side of the sound and end up at the Winslow ferry dock.

After dropping off Sandy's sisters at the drugstore, Jim drove to the Winslow supermarket. A solid, gray-haired woman sat at a table on the walkway between the store and the parking lot, sorting forms. She wore a T-shirt from last year's race, which proclaimed: *Annual Great Cross-Sound Rowing Race.* Sandy filled out forms for herself and Greg, entering them in the race and listing the size of their dinghies.

"How many people have signed up?" she asked.

The woman said, "Let's see, you're 87 and Greg is 88. Um. I'm sure we'll have 200 before we finish. Unless it pours."

"Can't stop Sandy with a little rain," Jim said. "She's been out rowing every day this summer, rain or shine."

The woman said, "I expect most of the rowers feel that way."

Sandy and Jim walked across the street to the paint store, bought another can of paint that Jim needed, and stopped at the drugstore to pick up Izzy and Andrea. They said hi to Marta, who was busy at the cash register, and then decided they had done all their errands in town.

"I don't suppose anyone would like a milkshake?" Jim asked.

"Yeah!" Andrea shouted and Izzy said, "That would be very nice, thank you."

They picked up milkshakes at the drive-in counter, then sat at the edge of the parking area where there were a half-dozen small tables with benches. Jim stretched out his tanned legs and picked at the paint flecks with his fingernails. Over the edge of her milkshake container Sandy watched the cars go by on the road, waving occasionally to friends who shouted her name. Izzy sat very quietly, concentrating on her shake, but occasionally glanced at Jim. Andrea jumped up and down, one minute standing, the next minute sitting.

Three of Izzy's school friends came out of the drive-in carrying cones, licking at the cone edges and the soft white ice cream that ran melting down their fingers. They said, "Hey, Izzy, whatcha doing in town?"

"My sister came in to sign up for the cross-sound race."

Their eyes widened. "You gonna be in the race, Sandy?"

"Right."

"You rowing all that way by yourself?"

"Sure am."

"What if you get too tired to finish?"

"We'll have a motor boat escort. But don't worry about me. I'll finish, all right."

"How about you, Jim?" they asked.

"Jimmy gets seasick," Andrea giggled.

Izzy scowled as though she were embarrassed by her younger sister's remark.

Jim made a face at them around the straw of his milkshake. One of the girls moved closer to Sandy and said, "My sister says that your boyfriend is Greg Johnson."

"The one who plays basketball?" another girl demanded.

The three girls drew together, raised their eyebrows, and exchanged glances, as though they weren't sure if they should ask Sandy about her boyfriend. Watching them, Sandy understood their confusion. She had felt that way about the whole subject of boys and dating, too, before she started high school. She remembered too well the junior high dances, when the boys stood at one end of the gym, fooling around and play-fighting with each other. Meanwhile, the girls either danced together or stood at the other end of the gym. They watched the boys with quick glances and tried to look as though they did not really want to be asked to dance. Sandy hadn't started dating until her third year in high school, and even then there had been no one special. Practically all of them were boys she had known since kindergarten, some of them members of committees she worked on. Until Greg, there had been no one she cared to think of as her "boyfriend."

Izzy's friends whispered among themselves until one blurted out, "Oh, you do, too, know, Silvie! He's the handsome one, real tall, with the foxy brown eyes!"

Sandy bit back a smile.

"Is that true?" one of the girls demanded of her.

Sandy tried to sound casual. "If you're talking about sunburned Greg Johnson, okay, I'll agree he's tall, and not bad looking, but I wouldn't know about the foxy part."

Jim, still bent forward, turned his head to glance up at her. "Greg has a sunburn?"

"Sure looked like it to me."

"Gee, that's rough. Going to make rowing hard."

"Sunburn or not, he's gorgeous," Izzy's friend insisted, and to Sandy's surprise, Izzy blushed.

Jim stood, picked up everyone's milkshake containers, and threw them in the trash can. Glaring at Izzy's friends, he said, "Let's go before I throw up."

Chapter 5

When Greg and Sandy went to a spy movie at the local theater the next night, Sandy fell asleep during the chase scene, sliding down slightly in the padded seat, her head falling towards her shoulder. Greg's hand tightened over hers. Sandy blinked, tried to watch the screen, and found dream thoughts weaving through the action — one moment the lighted motion filled her mind and the next moment she seemed to be riding in the chase car.

Finally she wedged herself in the seat, her elbow on the armrest, her head supported between her hand and the chair's back, and gave up struggling. When the film ended, the theater's dim blue wall lights flared and the overhead lighting came on.

Sandy woke long enough to stumble out of the theater into the dark evening where a misty rain brushed her face, clearing her mind. Hanging on to Greg's hand, she ran with him to the car, hurried into it, and brushed her hands over her hair to shake off the raindrops.

"Not the best movie I ever saw," Greg said as he backed out of the parking lot.

Chapter 5

"And not the worst," Sandy agreed, "but pretty close."

"How could you tell? You were asleep."

"Only for a minute!"

"Would you believe half an hour?"

"I was not! Was I?"

"Okay, quiz time. How many guys got shot before the cops reached the warehouse?"

Sandy frowned, trying to remember. "Don't know, do you?" Greg's profile was outlined by the dashboard lights. He turned, met her eyes, then looked back at the road. "Do you even remember the warehouse?"

"Okay," Sandy admitted, "tell me how it ended."

"I shouldn't but I'm a nice guy. Remember the short sergeant, the one with the mustache? Okay, he took the first car with the rookie, the Irish one, and then the big guy . . ."

Greg's voice droned on. Sandy tried to follow, tried to separate which guy was which, but slowly gave in to the weight of her eyelids. She shook her head, blinked hard, screwed her face around in an effort to stay awake, but none of it helped. She heard Greg talking, felt the swaying of the car, saw the occasional flashes of light from oncoming headlights, and even vaguely smelled the mingled odors of musty car interior and damp night air. The dull, vague ache of weary muscles spread across her shoulders, down her back, and along her legs.

When Greg grasped her shoulder to shake her awake, Sandy mumbled, "What is it?"

"We're home."

Peering into the darkness, Sandy saw the entry light on her house shining through the veil of rain. It lit an arched frame of fir branches around the house, but could not penetrate further, so that the surrounding woods disappeared into blackness.

"I'm sorry. I can't seem to stay awake."

"So I noticed." He sounded curt and Sandy felt guilty. She should have called off the date, told him she was too tired to go to the movies, but she had felt less tired after supper and thought that a spy movie would keep her awake.

"You want to come in and have some ice cream?" she asked.

"I guess not. I'm not hungry, and anyway, you'd probably fall asleep with the spoon in your mouth."

"Oh, come on, Greg! I promise not to fall asleep until I finish eating."

"And then?"

"Then I should probably stumble off to bed," she admitted. "I hate to tell you this, but I ache all over."

"That's what you get for rowing in the rain."

"You know some dry place I could have practiced this morning?"

"You could have slept-in this morning. You knew we were going out tonight."

Sandy said softly, "Don't be mad, Greg. You know I have to row every day. If I can't row in a little rain, what will I do if I get caught in a downpour in the race?"

"Same as you do in the sun. Keep rowing."

Chapter 5

"Sure, that's okay for you. You're probably in better shape than I am, but I don't dare miss a day."

"Listen, Sandy, it's like I told you. As long as you *know* you can row for two hours, you know you can make it across. Practicing every day won't make that much difference."

Sandy felt sure that Greg was wrong, but she didn't want to argue with him. It was up to him to practice. No matter how much she wanted him to practice with her, she had no right to push him. She touched his arm lightly, asking, "How's the sunburn?"

"Okay if you don't hug me too hard," he said, sliding his arms around her.

Where her hands rested lightly on his arms, she could feel the heat from his skin through his shirt. "I'm afraid to touch you."

"There's lots of me that isn't sunburned," he teased, and kissed her.

Sandy closed her eyes automatically, relaxing into Greg's arms, her hands sliding across his shoulders and around his neck.

He jerked away. "Ouch!"

Sandy's eyes flew open. "Are you all right?"

"Don't touch my shoulders! The rest of me is all yours, babe."

Sandy giggled.

"It isn't funny," he said, and Sandy clamped her hand over her mouth. She hadn't meant to laugh at him. It really was unfair that she was falling asleep and being such a lousy date on the same night that Greg was suffering from a sunburn. She remembered now that he had been squirming around in his seat in the movie, but she had been too sleepy at the time to notice or think about his burn.

"I'm sorry, Greg, I really am." She peered through the darkness and saw that he was smiling at her, his teeth and eyes a faint glow in the shadowed oval of his face. "I didn't mean to laugh."

He said, "I know. Hey, we'll make up for lost time Friday."

"Friday?"

"Party at Dudley's place. I'll pick you up around eight."

"I can't go to a party on Friday," Sandy said.

"Why not?"

"Greg! The race is Saturday!"

"Not until noon."

"Yeah, but — oh, Greg, I can't! I've got to get to bed early the night before, so I have time to get up and have breakfast and do some warm-ups, and then we've got to get our boats on the trucks — "

"We can load the boats Friday afternoon."

"Yeah, but we'll have to catch the ferry to Seattle and drive down to Alki Point and get the boats unloaded!"

"Don't worry, we'll get there."

Sandy felt a strange, sinking feeling inside. She knew, before she said another word, that if she didn't go to the party with him, he would have a hard time forgiving her. Yet, if she went to the party, she knew she would be too tired to do her best in the race. She had spent the whole summer practicing for it.

Sandy took a deep breath and said, "Greg, I don't want to choose between you and the race."

"I never asked you to! I'm going to be in the race, too, remember?"

"Yes, but — oh, Greg. I can't go to a party Friday night!"

"You mean you don't want to." He wasn't smiling now.

"Of course I want to go."

"Then go! We won't stay late. I'll get you home whenever you say."

"That won't work. I'll be ready to go to bed about the time the party is getting really started, and then you'll be mad because I want to leave."

"I don't get mad!" Greg exclaimed. "But what's so wrong with going to a party? We can't do anything, Sandy, because you've always got to practice. You're always too tired. You couldn't even stay awake in the movie. You weren't like this last spring."

"But it's only for another week and then it'll be over and I won't have to practice any more," Sandy said.

"And then it'll be something else."

"Like what?"

"I dunno, but it'll be something! You're always going to be too busy to have time for me."

"I *do* have time for you. I always have time for you. It's you who quit rowing with me," Sandy said, and heard her voice rise more than she had meant to let it.

"Oh sure, turn it around and blame it on me."

Sandy sat silently, meeting his gaze, but unable to say anything more. She had lost track of how the argument had begun and didn't really care. She had thought of Greg as her boyfriend, someone who belonged to her by some unwritten arrangement. Her friends recognized this when they said "Sandy-and-Greg" as though it were one word. Now she remembered that he didn't belong to her — tomorrow he could decide never to phone her again, never go out with her, never reach out to hold her.

Was the race worth that?

She said slowly, "Do you want me to drop out of the race?"

Greg didn't say anything for a long minute. Then he said, "No. I don't want that. Forget about the party. It's not important."

As soon as he said it, she knew it was important. She also knew that she could not drop out of the race even if he asked her to.

Sandy let out her breath slowly, knowing she had to stick to what she had started and go with the race. She said only, "I'm sorry about the party."

He leaned toward her, kissed her on the mouth, then reached past her to open the car door. "You better go in now, babe."

Sandy ran through the rain to the house, then turned back to wave. She could not see if he waved back. When he drove out of the driveway, the wheels of his car spun in the gravel as though he had stamped down on the accelerator, and she wondered if he had done that on purpose.

But he had kissed her good night. Well, that was something. If he had intended to break up with her, he would not have kissed her. After the race was over and she'd had a few days to rest up, maybe she could plan a beach party to make up for the one they would miss.

When she walked into the kitchen, there was a note on the refrigerator, under a magnet shaped like a miniature banana. It said, "Jim phoned. He says he can have the truck Saturday to take you to Alki. There's pie in the refrig. Help yourself. Mom."

Chapter 6

Jim drove his truck down the Winslow dock and onto the ferry. The ferry was a large, green-and-white state-owned boat that held two hundred cars and had an upper deck with a coffee shop and lounge area for the hundreds of walk-on passengers, as well as room for those who drove on.

Throughout the drive to the dock, Sandy kept turning around to stare out the back window of the truck cab, checking her dinghy to be sure they had tied it down tightly so that it wouldn't sway in the truck bed. They had to leave the tailgate down, letting the dinghy project behind the truck, with red-cloth warning flags tied to it. As they went down the ferry ramp onto the boat, she watched for Greg.

"See him?" Jim asked.

"I see a lot of other trucks hauling and towing boats, but I don't see Greg. He said he'd meet us on the ferry."

"Probably left home late. He'll make it."

"I guess so." Greg had phoned Friday night to wish her luck in the race. Sandy had asked him if he wanted her and Jim to stop by on the way to help him load his boat on his truck. But he had said no thanks, his dad would help him. He hadn't mentioned the party. Sandy could not bring herself to ask him if he planned to go without her. If he did, he did. He had to make his own decision about how much rest he needed before the race.

Anyway, if she asked, he might think she was worried that he would go with some other girl. There was no point letting him think that she was jealous or thought she owned him.

After the race, with the strain behind them, everything would be all right again. It just had to be.

When the ferry pulled away from the slip, Jim and Sandy wandered up and down the car deck, looking for Greg. His truck wasn't on the ferry. They finally stopped searching and stood at the railing, staring out at the dull gray sound for the rest of the half-hour ride. A misty rain hung above the water like a low cloud, cutting visibility and keeping the temperature in the low sixties.

"He'll catch the next ferry," Jim said.

"You think so?"

"Sure. The water's heavy, Sandy. It's going to be kind of rough."

Sandy studied the sound, its width at this point no more than seven miles, but its length extending northward past the horizon to the San Juan Islands and Canada. Merchant ships from around the world came from the Pacific through the wind-whipped Straits of Juan de Fuca, down the temperamental waters of the sound to the protected port of Seattle.

After the ferry docked in Seattle, Jim drove to

Alki Point where the race was to start. A number of other trucks pulled in with them. The water already held a jumble of boats, some trucked over, many towed across the water from Winslow by motorboats.

As the race organizers separated boats into classes and arranged starting times, Sandy looked with surprise at the wide variety of entries. There were many one-person boats, like her own, making up the largest class; but there were also doubles entries and some racing shells with crews. There were a few catchall classes with everything from a paddle-wheel, powered by a man on a bicycle, to a barge that held eight rowers dressed in slave costumes and a woman on a cushioned seat dressed like Cleopatra. The only limitation on the entries was that they must be human-powered.

A committee member, her face half-hidden behind a turned-up collar, handed Sandy a number patch. "Pin that on your back," she said. "You're number 53 now. What class are you in?"

"Women's singles," Sandy said.

"Okay, 53, you'll be in the sixth heat of your class. The starting line is midships of the judges' boats. Listen for your number for any instructions. Now, if you'll spell your name for me, I'll get you registered here and then you can launch your boat. Stay out of the race area until your heat is called."

A chill wind swirled across the sound, lifting the water into cross-hatch patterns, but not powerful enough to raise whitecaps. Sandy was glad of that. If the water was too rough, the race would be canceled.

Chapter 6

After Jim pinned Sandy's number to her parka, they carried her dinghy from the truck, settled it in the water, and added Sandy's backpack containing her thermos, a snack, plus an extra sweater.

Pulling her hood up over her head, Sandy climbed into her boat. Jimmy said good-bye, adding, "Don't forget your line."

Sandy leaned over to fasten a length of fishing line to the stern of her dinghy, a line complete with bobbin and a light weight of lead. With the line and bobbin, she knew that she could stay on a straight course for the Winslow harbor just by keeping her eye on the line. As long as the bobbin dragged straight out behind her boat, she would know she had not changed course. If it began to pull to either side, she could then turn her head to sight the harbor and correct her course.

"You're sure that'll work?" Greg had asked when she explained it to him.

"I tried it around the rock."

"Sure, but there's no current in the bay. The sound is different."

"All I can do is try," she had said. Now she wondered if he would bring a line for his boat, or even if he would arrive in time to enter the race.

After almost a half-hour wait, the loudspeaker announced, "Women's singles, sixth heat!"

"That's me," Sandy thought as she rowed toward the starting area. She tried to visualize the imaginary line between the midships of the two large white judges' cruisers, swinging her dinghy around so that her bow would be as close to that starting line as possible.

Over a bullhorn a judge shouted, "Number 47,

you've crossed the start! Get back! Hey, there, 32, you too, get back! Come on, you're holding us up!"

While the offending boats back-paddled, Sandy scanned the shore. To her relief, she saw Greg and his father hurrying toward the water, carrying Greg's dinghy. At the same time, he saw her.

Greg shouted, "Good luck!" Although the wind carried away the sound of his voice, Sandy could see the words on his mouth.

The loudspeaker crackled, announcing the sixth heat. Sandy's grip tightened. She edged slowly toward the line, watching the judge's arm rise, afraid she would drift across the start too soon and be called back. Her stomach lurched from nervousness.

The gun went off.

Sandy pulled away from the start with her class, concentrating on maintaining a steady stroke and trying to ignore the other entrants. Immediately she felt the difference in the water. Here, off the open point, a current fought with her oars.

Some of the other rowers moved rapidly past her, their oars churning the water at a fast, frantic pace that she thought they could not maintain for long. Others lagged behind. All around, more boats moved at her speed. An escort of motorboats stayed well to the side, but always within sight in case anyone needed aid.

Sandy settled into her own pattern, keeping her strokes at the pace she had practiced daily, all summer long. She smiled to herself, remembering Greg comparing her to the turtle in the children's story of the tortoise and the hare. She wasn't any tortoise. She was definitely moving ahead of some of the boats and rowing with fair speed, considering the choppy water. What she could not predict was how well she would be able to maintain her pace in the rougher waters of the sound, having only practiced in her protected bay.

Sandy could see the next heat, following hers. Greg would not be in that one, but he might be in the one after it, depending on the time he signed in and the arrangement of the heats. Only the race organizers could have any real idea of where everyone was, as they carefully checked in entrants and assigned numbers.

Several times Sandy glanced around, but the other boats were dark, unidentifiable shapes on the gray sound. Mist surrounded her and numbed her fingers. She had tried several times to row while wearing gloves, but she could not find gloves that gave her as firm a grip as her own callused palms.

As soon as he had finished helping her launch her boat, Jim had raced back to his truck to drive from Alki to the ferry terminal to catch the ferry back to Winslow. Now to the north Sandy saw the huge white shape of the ferry, with its lighted windows, gliding through the fog toward Winslow. Jimmy would be on it, staring out, trying to spot her boat and Greg's.

Sandy checked her watch. Half an hour. After resting her oars in her boat, she dug out her hiker's mix of nuts and raisins and poured hot cider into her thermos lid. The warmth of the cider flowed through her, a comfort against the chill wind. She wondered if Greg had remembered to carry a thermos.

After checking her course, she lowered the oars to the water and continued to row. Her boat had drifted almost to a standstill, bobbing on the choppy surface. Clenching the oars, she threw her weight into her stroke to regain momentum. Despite the cold, Sandy felt streams of perspiration running down her back beneath her shirt and parka, but she knew better than to remove any of her layers of clothing. The mist swirls would cut right through her body heat, tightening her muscles and possibly causing them to cramp.

When Sandy passed a boat that had pulled out in front of her at the beginning of the race, she saw its rower sitting motionless, head in hands, while the oars dragged untended. The rower was obviously exhausted. At least Sandy wouldn't make that mistake. With months of practice behind her, she thought she had the stamina to reach the Winslow dock, if she didn't push too hard. Maybe she would be the last boat in, but she would get there on her own. That, she had decided early in the summer, was the only goal she would set for herself. As there were no practice races and no way to know who would enter or what sort of experience the other entrants would have, she had made up her mind that she would compete only with herself.

Greg had joked that they would sweep the field, with him winning men's singles and Sandy winning women's.

"Yeah, sure," she had agreed, laughing, but she had not really cared. She knew that for Greg, who had been very competitive in basketball, winning meant beating someone else. For Sandy it meant reaching her goal. To that extent, she was determined to win.

The woman in the near boat lifted her head and waved to the escort boat to pick her up. As Sandy's strokes lengthened the distance between them, she saw the motorboat move in toward the other boat and toss a line.

She glanced around through the fog, wondering if any other boats had dropped out. During the hour that they had been on the water, the entrants had spread farther apart. Many of them were beyond her vision in the wet gray cloud and she could not tell what they were doing. She wished she could spot Greg.

She rowed automatically, watching the oars rise and fall, until her vision narrowed to her own boat, walling her into a gray tunnel of fog. She heard her own breathing, the creak of her oarlocks, the slapping of the water on the hull, the breaking of the water's surface with the oars— even the spattering of the rainlike drops from their tips.

Her trance broke when she noticed the bobbin swinging north on its length of fishing line beyond the stern.

Had she gone off course? Turning to look over her shoulder, Sandy peered through the mist and saw the rock that marked the entrance to the Winslow harbor. She was still on course. The wind-ruffled water, or perhaps a current, drew her bobbin. She had not turned.

Resting her oars, Sandy had another snack, then bent into her stroke with new energy, knowing that she could not stop again. She felt so chilled that she had to keep moving to prevent shivering. Her hands were so numb that she could not feel the wood beneath her fingers, but the aching in her knuckles ran all the way up her arms to her shoulders, back down her spine, and through her legs.

Puget Sound was no Sunset Bay. Although she had rowed for longer stretches of time, she had never rowed against rough water, its surges straining at her oars. Even though this was August, the fog managed to cut all warmth from the sun, seeping beneath her parka, chilling her skin where a moment earlier she had perspired, and causing her jeans to cling damply to her legs. Her oarlocks creaked so loudly, they almost sounded as though they were protesting, too. Maybe the whole race was a dumb idea, she thought, wondering why she had spent a whole summer practicing for it when she could have been swimming and sunbathing and going to parties with Greg.

"No wonder he thinks I'm nuts," she muttered to herself. "I hope he doesn't feel as miserable now as I do. I wouldn't blame him if he didn't speak to me for days."

As her boat turned past the point of land at the harbor's edge, it slid into quieter water where the surface barely ruffled. The surrounding cliffs, with their stands of fir, caught the wind and slowed its pace. To her surprise, she could now smell the fragrance of trees beyond the sea smells that had filled her senses during the crossing. Cormorants rose — black, awkward shapes — from a nearby sandspit.

Sandy glanced over her shoulder, saw the dock, and forgot her weariness in a glow of excitement. She increased her pace, anxious to finish. With the dock in sight she thought she could even cut a minute or two off her time.

Greg would be finishing, too, or perhaps he had passed her and was already in. Her parents and Jim would be on the dock. Above the harbor she could see people standing out on their porches, waving. Sandy managed to lift a hand and wave back. After the race they would all go to the picnic, compare their aches, calluses, and blisters, and laugh about their doubts in the middle of the choppy, fog-shrouded sound.

As Sandy passed the judges' float that marked the finish line, a man shouted, "What's your number?"

For a second her mind went blank. Then she called back, "53," turning her shoulder so that he could see it. He waved and smiled, then bent over his clipboard to record her time. Later the judges would compare finishing times with starting times, sort the entrants by their numbers into their classes, and determine the winners.

Exhausted, Sandy rowed slowly toward the floating dock near the head of the harbor. As her dinghy pulled alongside the dock, she heard Jim shout, "How's your time, Sandy? How's your time?"

Sandy shouted her starting time to him, then

checked her watch. She had covered the course in about an hour and a half, slower than last year's winners, she knew, but not bad.

Jim raced down the ramp to pull her dinghy against the floating dock and hold it still while she tossed her oars on the dock and climbed out.

"You're going to be awfully close to the top," Jim said.

Too weary to think about it, Sandy sat down on the dock and watched the other boats pull in. They bobbed in the water, tied to their pilings, impossible to identify. They could be entrants in men's or women's, singles or crew, and they would have to wait for the race committee to determine finishing times for the now deserted boats.

Jim handed her a towel. When Sandy finished rubbing the mist from her hands and face, he pressed a steaming paper container of coffee into her numb fingers. To her surprise, Sandy realized she was shivering violently.

Jim draped a blanket around her shoulders.

"You're a regular first aid station," Sandy said through chattering teeth.

"You'll feel better in a minute."

"I feel better already. Seen Greg?"

"Well, yeah."

"He's finished?"

"He's around someplace."

Sandy stared up at Jim, demanding, "How did he do?"

Jim shrugged and looked over her head to the incoming boats. "Greg — well — he got towed in. I guess — I guess it's pretty rough out there today, huh?"

Chapter 6

"Towed in? He didn't finish on his own?" Sandy felt as though her heart had dropped down to her feet. She knew how depressed and upset Greg would be.

"It's — he looked like he felt kind of sick."

Sandy stood slowly, handing Jim the coffee. She could not think of anything to say. While she tried to arrange her thoughts to better understand what had happened, she raised her arms above her head and did a few stretches.

"Stiff?" Jim asked, then laughed. "Guess that's a dumb question."

"Nothing like I'll be tomorrow," Sandy said.

"That's for sure."

Over Jim's shoulder she saw Greg walking down the ramp toward her. Her thoughts scrambled in a dozen directions, trying to come up with something to say to him. If she had been towed in, she didn't think there was anything anyone could say that would make her feel better about it.

Greg said, "So you made it. Good for you." He forced a smile.

"It was really rough," Sandy said, her eyes searching his, trying to read his thoughts. Greg nodded.

"I didn't expect that much wind. I mean, with all that fog. It's usually calmer in fog," Sandy stammered. "I — I thought about quitting — almost — a couple times."

Greg still didn't say anything.

A voice over a loudspeaker said, "Okay, we now have best time for the women's division."

Sandy stiffened, listening. Jim's eyes widened, waiting. Greg stared down at the dock.

The voice said, "Okay, here it is. What's — oh — right." The speaker faded, crackled, then the voice boomed out, "Yes, here it is. Okay, folks, best time in women's singles is one hour and twenty-six minutes, eighteen seconds."

Sandy held her breath. If that was winning, she should be near the top dozen because she was sure she was under an hour and a half, though she didn't know exactly.

"One hour, twenty-six minutes, eighteen seconds," the voice repeated. "Winning time set by Sandy Stevens! Sandy Stevens! Is she around?"

Sandy's mouth dropped open.

Greg muttered, "Good for you, babe," and walked away.

Jim threw his arms around Sandy, pinning her arms to her sides, and half-lifted her off the dock. He shouted, "Hurray for you, Sandy!"

Sandy laughed, wriggled loose, hugged him back, and then jumped up and down on the dock, hugging herself.

The loudspeaker said, "I see a lot of rowers wandering off. I know you're cold. Sorry we couldn't order the weather. But don't forget to come back to the park this afternoon for the salmon feed. We want to announce all the winners for all the classes, and we'll have the times, plus more than you can eat. If you haven't picked up your T-shirt, we've still got some left, so you can get it then. Okay, we have a lot more boats coming in and as soon as we get more times, we'll announce them." The speaker crackled off.

"First!" Jim shouted. "Sandy, you're first! I *knew* you'd win!"

"You *knew*? For a while out there, I didn't even know if I'd finish," she shouted back at him. She didn't know why she was shouting, but somehow she couldn't bring her voice down to mere talking.

"I knew you would," he insisted. "You can do anything you set your mind to."

"I can't believe it," Sandy laughed. Her body ached. Her hands were raw and trembling with cold. Yet all she wanted to do was giggle. She tried to turn her thoughts to her boat, knowing it still had to be lifted out of the water, or even to Greg, knowing she really should run after him to comfort him, but she could do none of that. She stood grinning, dazed.

A crowd of people gathered around her, congratulating her, patting her shoulders, and then her parents and sisters pushed through the crowd and hugged and kissed her.

"Stop," Sandy begged, still giggling, "or you'll all make me cry."

Chapter 7

After everyone wandered off to watch the other boats, Jim found Frank and Marta in the crowd. They helped carry Sandy's gear to the truck.

"I can do that," Sandy protested weakly, but they laughed at her.

"Just get yourself up to the truck," they said. "We don't mind carrying the dinghy, but we sure don't want to carry you."

She followed slowly behind them. As she walked up the slope to the parking area, she saw Greg sitting in his car, staring straight ahead at the next row of parked cars. Sandy went over to him and leaned down to the open window.

"Hi," she said.

He turned his head slowly, as though he didn't want to meet her gaze. His expression was blank, telling her nothing.

Sandy wanted to reach out, put her hand on his shoulder, and tell him how sorry she was that he hadn't been able to finish. But she didn't know how to say it. Anything she said now would hurt him more. She asked, "Are you going to the salmon bake?"

"No, I don't think so."

"Oh. Uh — Frank and Marta are going. Maybe — maybe we can do something tomorrow . . ." Her voice trailed off, uncertain. Then she tried to make a joke. "If I get up tomorrow. I may sleep through next week."

Greg didn't answer.

Sandy blurted, "Hey, Greg, a lot of people didn't finish. It was rough out there."

"You finished." His voice was flat.

"Yeah, well, I was lucky."

Greg turned his face away from her, concentrating on fitting his key into the ignition. "Was that it? Luck?"

"I — I guess. Besides — you had a sunburn. It's hard to row with a sunburn."

"I don't need you to make excuses for me."

"I'm not — I only meant, Greg, I'm sorry."

"Me, too. I wish I'd never entered that stupid race."

Sandy almost said, "I'm not sorry about that," but pressed her lips together in time.

After another long silence, Greg said, "It was a dumb idea. I don't know why I ever bothered. What's such a big deal about rowing across the stupid sound? It's not like there's any prize money or anything."

"It's just for fun." Sandy tried to smile.

Greg looked up at her, his eyes narrowed. "You've got some weird ideas about what's fun, you know that?"

Sandy exclaimed, "I thought it was fun! I enjoyed it. That doesn't mean you have to. We don't have to like the same things."

"What's that supposed to mean?"

"Nothing! I mean, you don't have to row if you don't want to. It doesn't have anything to do with — " Sandy heard her voice rising with irritation. She took a breath and said more softly, "I mean, we can like different things and still like each other, can't we?"

Greg shrugged. "Yeah, sure, babe. Well, see ya around." After starting his car, he looped his elbow over the seat back and turned away from Sandy to watch through his rear window.

Sandy stepped away from the car. He backed out of his parking space, shifted into drive, and left the parking lot. He didn't glance back or wave.

When Sandy reached the truck, Jim waited in the cab for her. Smiling, he asked, "Ready?"

Sandy forced herself to smile back.. "Sure."

"You still look cold. We've got time to run home before the picnic. Want to get dry clothes?"

"Could we? I'd really like to take a hot shower."

Jim drove out to the highway and headed north. The fog had floated upward, ribbon wisps still drifting through the treetops to the west. Overhead the clouds were transparent, almost like white mesh with a bright blue sky shining above it. The highway's surface was already dry, although the ferns that edged it still glittered with mist in the forest's shadow.

Sandy thought she should be laughing or singing, or at least exploding inside with excitement. But all she could feel was this heavy, damp emptiness, as though the fog had penetrated right through to her heart. Finishing the race had been so important to her all summer, a goal she had been willing to work at every day to reach. And now that she had not only finished, but actually come in first, she felt hollow. This wasn't the way she had thought it would be at all. But when she had daydreamed, she had imagined herself on the Winslow dock with Greg, both of them happy.

She said, "Jimmy, if you'd been in the race and couldn't finish, would you be mad because I did?"

Jim said, "You're asking me to answer for Greg. I can't do that."

"No, I'm not. I already know how Greg feels. But how would you feel?"

"It's kind of hard to say."

"Try."

Jim watched the road, but Sandy could tell, from the way the muscles in his square face tightened, that he was thinking. Finally he said, "When I got an A in algebra and you got a B, did that make you mad?"

"Of course not! You're better in algebra. And anyhow, I got an A in history and you got a C."

"Uh-huh."

"Did that make you mad?"

"You bet. I was mad at myself. But I wasn't mad at you."

"That's not quite the same thing as being in a race, though, is it?" Sandy said. "How do you feel when I always beat you at Monopoly?"

"You win because you cheat!"

"I don't! How could I? How can anybody cheat at Monopoly?"

"Loaded dice?"

"That's crazy!"

Jim laughed. "Yeah, okay. Look, Sandy, Greg's not mad at you. He's mad at himself. He knows why he didn't finish same as I know why I got a C. He didn't practice. While you were working at it, he was sleeping. He knows that. So quit worrying."

"It's hard to," Sandy admitted.

"He won't stay mad. He'll forget about it in a couple days."

They turned into Sandy's drive. While she pulled her gear out of the back, Jim untied the ropes on the dinghy. Together they slid it off the truck and carried it onto the lawn. After setting it down, Sandy rubbed her hands on her jeans.

She said, "I'm kind of tired. Maybe — why don't you go on to the picnic without me?"

"You're not going?"

"I — I don't think so." What fun would the picnic be without Greg, Sandy thought.

Jim pushed nonchalantly on his sweat shirt cuffs, arranging them around his elbows, then pulling them to his wrists. Without looking at her, he said, "A lot of people will feel let down if you're not there. I mean, they expect the winners to be there. Uh — why don't you go stand in a hot shower for a while and get warm? I'm in no hurry."

"I don't like to make you wait that long," Sandy said.

"I already told you I would. Hey, anyway, my shoes are wet. I'll go home and change them and then come back, okay?"

"Oh, I don't know . . ." Sandy mumbled, undecided.

"If you still don't want to go when I get back, okay, but I won't go if you don't." Without giving her a chance to argue, Jim jogged across the neighbors' lawns toward his house, leaving his truck in Sandy's driveway.

Sandy walked slowly to the house, shivering inside her damp clothes, unsure what she wanted to do. Jim was right, of course. Everyone would expect her to be at the picnic. Her parents would be there waiting for her. As she stood in the shower, letting the steam rise and the heat soak through her tired muscles, she tried to decide what she should do. If she went to the picnic, would she find herself standing around feeling unhappy because Greg wasn't there? This wasn't the way she had dreamed things would be at all.

On the other hand, she hadn't entered the race just to have something to do with Greg. She had entered it because she wanted to row across the sound. She had practiced every day because she loved rowing, loved the smells and sounds of the water, loved the steady rhythm of bending to her stroke.

And it wasn't as though Greg were the only person involved in the race. Her parents had made allowances, often helping her with her chores because they knew she was tired from practicing. Her sisters had learned to keep themselves busy and fix their own breakfasts while she was on the water. Jim had shown up almost every day to help her pull in her boat. They had all cheered her on, all summer long, believing in what she was doing.

Jim was right. No matter how she felt, she should go to the picnic. Just because Greg was disappointed was no reason for Sandy to disappoint everyone else. She would go, she decided, and she would try to act happy and excited because she owed that to her family and friends and probably even to the people who had worked hard to put the race together.

Sandy pulled on dry jeans and her Great Annual Cross-Sound Race T-shirt, ran a brush through her wavy black hair, forced herself to smile, and hurried outside to meet Jim. He was obviously relieved when he saw her.

"Come on," she said, trying to sound cheerful, "I'm hungry enough to eat a whole salmon."

"Some of those salmon weigh twenty pounds," he said.

"Lead me to 'em!"

At the picnic she found herself surrounded by people congratulating her. At first Sandy had to work to keep the corners of her mouth turned up. Her glance kept wandering past the crowds, hoping to find Greg. But soon she found herself smiling without trying as she answered questions.

"Yeah, it was foggy. I could see a couple of other boats but not many. No, I didn't get hungry. Yes, I took a snack mix, one of those hiker's mixes, you know, with raisins and carob chips and stuff. Yeah, I had a thermos. For *sure* I'll go again next year!"

Jim handed her a paper plate with smoked

salmon and baked beans and salad and roasted corn, all running deliciously into the buttered French bread. They sat on the ground, away from the tree shadows, where the sun had dried the grass. The smoke from the barbecue filled the air with its tantalizing smells of burning wood and roasting food. Sandy's family and friends milled around, carrying plates, shouting hello and congratulating everyone they bumped into — whether they were winners, losers, race organizers, cooks, or just spectators.

Marta sat down on the other side of Sandy and asked, "Greg coming?"

"I don't think so," Sandy said. "I wish he would. It's a lot of fun."

"Not for him."

"I guess not. I'm sorry he feels so bad about it."

Marta said, "The only thing that'd make Greg feel better is if you'd dropped out, too."

Sandy stared at her, speechless.

Marta shrugged. "It's true. Some guys can't stand to have a girl do anything better."

"I can't go around pretending to do everything worse than he does!" Sandy exclaimed.

"Me neither," Marta said and bit into her corn-on-the-cob.

On the other side of Sandy, Jim said, "Neat picnic, huh?"

Sandy grinned at him. "Yeah. Fantastic."

"You've got butter running down your chin."

Sandy wiped it away on her wrist, then searched for something with which to dry her wrist.

"Anything but the T-shirt," Jim said.

She smiled down at her new T-shirt. "Wouldn't dream of it. I may frame this thing and hang it on my wall."

"I would," Marta agreed.

Sandy saw her parents moving out of the crowd, leading a friend toward her. Her mother's smile almost matched her father's grin, it was so wide.

Her mother said, "Hazel, this is my daughter. I don't think you've met Sandy. Sandy won the women's division today. Sandy, are they going to announce the winners again?"

"They've already announced them three times," Sandy said.

"Oh. Well, Sandy, this is Mrs. Cavanaugh."

When Sandy said hello, Mrs. Cavanaugh held out her hand and told Sandy that she had known her mother for years at work and heard so much about Sandy, it was practically like having her own relative win, she was so proud.

Andrea shoved her way through the adults to flop down next to Jim. She said in her high, clear voice, "If they keep talking like that, Sandy's gonna get a swelled head!"

"Aren't you proud of her?" Jim asked.

Andrea pretended to think about his question, pulling her face into a frown, then giggled and said, "Yes."

"Don't act so dumb," Izzy whispered as she carefully found a place on the ground and tucked her feet under her legs as she sat down. To Sandy she whispered, "Is Greg here?"

Sandy whispered back, "I haven't seen him."

"Poor Greg," Izzy said, and Sandy felt sorry

for him all over again, realizing that, considering the size of the community, everyone would know he'd been towed in.

"Did Greg get sick?" Andrea demanded.

Sandy said yes, nothing more, not wanting to talk about Greg.

Andrea said, "Too bad. Hey, can I borrow your T-shirt sometime?"

"No way! This is my trophy!"

"But two hundred people have the same one," Andrea pointed out, "so it isn't such a big deal."

"It is to me," Sandy said. "It means I am one of two hundred very special people."

"One of the best of two hundred," Jim corrected. "Imagine that, a celebrity in my neighborhood."

Chapter 8

Sandy edged her dinghy into the dock. The dark bay glittered in the shade of the madronas, its surface dotted with tiny white seedpods from the trees. Jim reached out, caught the bow, and held her dinghy against the dock while she lifted her oars free of the locks and climbed out.

"Only fifty more weeks until the next race," Jim said. "You gonna be ready?"

"Laugh if you want, but I'll be back next year to defend my title."

"I know you will. You're like all the big winners. Once you're in the big time, it goes to your head, and you won't quit until old age forces you to retire."

Sandy laughed and intentionally bumped into him, her arms outstretched as though she were trying to keep her balance while shouldering her oars, her back banging into his chest.

Jim wavered on the dock's edge, tried to regain his balance, spun his arms, caught Sandy's elbow, and pulled them both off the dock.

They splashed into the water. Beneath the warm August sky, the bay was icy.

Chapter 8

Sandy came up gasping. "Hey, my oars! Get my oars!"

While she swam after one floating oar, Jim went after the other. Laughing and spitting out water, Sandy tossed her oar on the dock, then pulled herself up after it. Salt water streamed from her hair and T-shirt and shorts. Jim climbed up beside her, sat with his feet dangling in the water, and gasped for breath.

"What'd you do that for?" he demanded. Water rivulets ran from his T-shirt to the frayed edges of his cutoffs and down his tanned legs. His blond hair stuck to his square face, half-covering his eyes.

"I didn't think you'd fall," Sandy admitted. "I only meant to give you a scare."

"Some friend! I ought to let you pull in your own boat."

"Okay, I owe you one."

Jim cocked his head and peered at her from under the wet fringe of hair. His eyes sparkled, the laugh lines fanning out from their edges. "How much do you owe me?"

"Got something in mind?"

"Yeah. I've been so tied up with paint jobs, I never did finish painting our own porch. I'd like to get it finished before school starts."

"School! I wish you hadn't mentioned it. Aaaugh. Rush to catch the bus, rush to class, rush to lunch, rush back to class, rush to get the bus home. Yuk."

"All good things must end," Jim said solemnly.

Sandy socked his arm. "Spare me your philosophy."

"Why, Sandy Stevens! I am amazed at you. Do you think life is all play, no work?"

"I'll vote for that," Sandy said. "Come on, let's go get some lunch. We can bring it down here on the dock and sit in the sun until we dry out. Then I'll help you paint your porch."

They wandered slowly up the lawn to Sandy's house, avoiding stepping on rocks with their bare feet. In the dark shadows of the firs, the hydrangeas glowed sky blue, their huge flower heads drooping with their own weight. Swallows darted beneath the eaves.

Izzy called from the kitchen, "I got the sandwiches made!"

Andrea ran to the porch door shouting, "I made half!"

Glancing down at the puddle forming around her feet on the steps, Sandy said, "Want to bring them down to the dock?"

Andrea's eyes widened. "Wow! How did you get so wet?"

"We had a small accident," Sandy said.

"She pushed me in," Jim said.

"You didn't have to pull me with you!"

"Don't argue. It's not nice," Andrea said, and ran back to the kitchen.

Sandy looked straight into Jim's eyes, her mouth pulled down into a severe frown. "Andrea is right. It is not nice to fight. Now behave yourself."

Jim reached out quickly and tickled her ribs. Sandy doubled over giggling, then straightened, her arm raised to swing at him, but he had already dashed away and was hurrying down the dock ramp, his knees turned out in the funny gait that Sandy remembered since they were small.

"I'll get even!" she shouted.

"Good! Then you'll owe me two days' painting!"

Inside the house the phone rang. Sandy shouted to Andrea to answer it. Leaning against the screen door, she waited for Izzy to bring out the lunch.

Andrea padded out to the porch, her bare feet making a soft, thudding sound, her eyes wide as though she had a secret to share. "It's for you. It sounds like Greg. He hasn't called for a long time, has he?"

With a shrug, Sandy stepped down to the lawn, tried to wring as much water as possible from her shorts and shirt by twisting their edges between her fingers, wiped her feet dry on the grass, and then slowly went into the house to pick up the phone. She waved Andrea away and waited until she had disappeared into the kitchen before saying hello. She hoped her voice sounded light and friendly, as it would to any friend, and not anxious or upset. She did not want him to think that she had been waiting for him to call.

"Hi, babe," Greg said. "—uh—there's a party Saturday at Marshall's. You wanna go?"

He didn't mention that he had not phoned her for two weeks. Sandy wasn't really surprised. What could he say, except admit that he had been angry with her for that long, angry because she had done well in the race and he had not? He had to think about that for two weeks before deciding he would like to talk to her again, Sandy thought. She stood with the phone receiver in her hand and stared out of the window. She could not imagine herself staying angry with anyone for two weeks, though perhaps she might if she had a really good reason. As far as she could determine, he didn't have a reason at all. She had argued about that with herself during many an idle moment. She had thought it through as she slowly rowed around the rock each morning. At times, she had even thought of calling him, but what could she say? "I'm sorry you're angry because I did well in the race and you didn't?" That would hardly make him feel better.

Sandy hesitated, then said, "I — I don't think so, Greg."

Through the window she could see Jim stretched out full length on the weathered boards, his face resting on his crossed arms, as though he had been sleeping there for hours, his hair and clothes already beginning to dry in the sunshine. He had mentioned a movie in town on Saturday night, offering to take Izzy and Andrea along, if Sandy wanted to see it.

"You doing something else that night?" Greg asked.

If she told Jim that Greg had phoned and she was going to a party with him Saturday, what would Jim say?

He wouldn't say anything. He'd shrug and say okay and tomorrow when she came back from rowing, he would probably still meet her and pull in her boat. There was nothing she could do that would make Jim decide not to speak to her for two weeks. He would always be her friend.

To Greg, she said, "I just — I can't go. But thanks for asking me. It's nice to hear from you."

On the other end, Greg said, "Oh." He sounded surprised, as though he had expected her to jump at the chance to see him again. "Ah — well — maybe Sunday? You want to go out Sunday?"

Sandy said, "No, I don't think so."

"Are you trying to tell me to get lost?"

"No! No, I don't mean that, Greg."

"Want to try the 'let's just be friends' line?"

Sandy sucked in her breath and held it while she thought. If she turned him down now, he would not call again. Or would he? Would she sit around for another two weeks waiting for him to change his mind? And if he did change, would she find herself tiptoeing around his feelings, always wondering if he would be upset by something she did? She said slowly, "Something like that."

"I thought we were more than friends."

"I did, too, I guess. Only now — you're making this kind of hard."

There was a long silence on the line. She could see Greg in her imagination, his tall shape, his handsome face, his dark eyes, and slow, teasing smile. There were so many things about Greg that she liked, but at the same time, she knew they weren't right for each other.

Finally Greg said, "Right. See you around," and hung up.

Sandy hung up the receiver and let her breath out slowly, surprised to discover that she had been holding it in while she waited for him to answer. In an odd way she felt relieved, as though she had finished an exam and it hadn't been as difficult as she had expected it to be.

When she reached the dock, she sat down beside Jim. He turned his head and glanced up at her.

"Greg phoned," she said. If she didn't tell him, Andrea would mention it and he would think she had not wanted him to know. It didn't matter if he knew. They had never really had secrets from each other.

Jim stared out at the water. "Yeah?"

"He wanted me to go to a party Saturday night."

Sandy saw the muscles tighten across Jim's shoulders but all he said was, "Are you going?"

With a shock, she heard the slight edge of anger in his tone. Where had her head been all summer, she wondered, watching him, and finally realizing how he felt about her. Why hadn't she noticed before?

Sandy would be the first one to admit that she had never been the kind of person who went around analyzing people. Her mother occasionally said that she wasn't very sensitive, but that was when she did something to upset one of her sisters and didn't realize she had done it until they started to cry. Then she always felt terrible.

Now, she thought to herself, she could understand what her mother meant. She must have been blind, all those mornings when Jim met her at the dock, all those times when he begged off from going to parties that she went to with Greg.

What would the summer have been without

Jim? She would have done her practicing alone, had no one to discuss her plans with, had no one to share the excitement of the race. It hadn't been Greg who had made the summer so special, had it, she asked herself.

Sandy said firmly, "Of course I'm not going to the party. I'm going to the movies with you, remember?"

Jim rolled over on his back and grinned up at her.

Sandy grinned back. "Or are you taking back your invitation?"

The screen door banged shut behind Izzy and Andrea as they struggled out of the house balancing trays of plates and glasses and a lemonade pitcher. From across the lawn their voices carried clearly, arguing over who had the heaviest tray and who had done the most work getting together the lunch.

Sandy said, "And we don't have to take my sisters with us." She spoke softly, so that only Jim would hear her.

He said, "I don't mind."

"I know you don't. That's why we're not taking them this time. Okay?"

His grin widened. "If you think I'm going to argue with that, you're crazy."